NIGHTSHADES

NOVELS BY BILL PRONZINI

"Nameless Detective" Novels

Nightshades
Quicksilver
Bindlestiff
Casefile (collection)
Dragonfire
Scattershot
Hoodwink
Labyrinth
Twospot (with Collin Wilcox)
Blowback
Undercurrent
The Vanished
The Snatch

Other Novels

The Eye (with John Lutz)
Starvation Camp
The Gallows Land
Masques
The Cambodia File (with Jack Anderson)
Prose Bowl (with Barry N. Malzberg)
Night Screams (with Barry N. Malzberg)
Acts of Mercy (with Barry N. Malzberg)
Games
The Running of Beasts (with Barry N. Malzberg)
Snowbound
Panic!
The Stalker

Nonfiction

Gun in Cheek

NIGHTSHADES

A "Nameless Detective" Mystery

BILL PRONZINI

St. Martin's Press
New York

 For information, address St. Martin's Press, 175 Fifth Avenue, New York, N.Y. 10010.

Design by Andy Carpenter

Pronzini, Bill.
Nightshades.

I. Title.
PS3566.R67N5 1984 813′.54 83-26721
ISBN 0-312-57338-3

First Edition
10 9 8 7 6 5 4 3 2 1

This One is For Bob Randisi—An Eye for an Eye's

NIGHTSHADES

ONE

Barney Rivera said cheerfully, "The name of the place is Ragged-Ass Gulch."

I just looked at him.

"Well, that was the name it was born with, anyhow," he said. "Back in the days of the Gold Rush. Nowadays it's called Musket Creek."

"Uh-huh. And nowadays it's a ghost town?"

"Sort of. Sixteen people live there."

"Uh-huh," I said again. "Where did you say it was?"

"Trinity County, north of Weaverville."

"That's not Mother Lode country."

"Not exactly, no. Everybody thinks the Gold Rush was limited to the Mother Lode, but in the early eighteen-fifties it raged up around Mount Shasta too. Ragged-Ass Gulch was a real boom town in those days."

"Why Ragged-Ass Gulch?" I asked him. "The name, I mean."

He shrugged. "Who knows? Miners used to give towns names like that back then. You know, colorful. Whiskeytown, Lousy Ravine, Bogus Thunder, Git-Up-And-Git—names like that."

"You been doing some homework, huh, Barney?"

"You know me," he said. "Conscientious to a fault."

Well, I did know him and he *was* conscientious. I'd thought at first that he might be putting me on a little, because he had a somewhat flaky sense of humor, but what he'd been giving me was straight goods. He had my attention, too, in spite of myself. I had come here out of professional courtesy, with half a mind to turn down whatever job he offered me, no matter what it was; I was planning to leave on vacation tomorrow, Friday. But it takes a different and less romantic type than me not to be interested in a case involving a semi-ghost town with the slightly bawdy name of Ragged-Ass Gulch.

We were sitting in Barney's office at the San Francisco branch of Great Western Insurance. The office was on the twenty-ninth floor of one of the buildings in the Embarcadero Center, and through the windowed wall behind his desk you could see all the way across the Bay to Mount Diablo. Or you could have if a thickish haze hadn't been choking off some of the early May sunshine and obliterating parts of Oakland and the other East Bay cities. It was a nice view, and a nice office, too, as befitted Great Western's chief claims adjustor.

Barney himself fit the title just fine; in addition to being conscientious, he was shrewd, tenacious, and healthily skeptical. The only thing wrong with him was that he didn't *look* like a chief claims adjustor. Maybe it was just me; maybe I had seen *Double Indemnity* too many times and I expected all claims adjustors to look like Edward G. Robinson playing Keyes, or at least Fred MacMurray as Walter Neff. But here was Barney, five feet two in his stocking feet, tubby, with a mop of unruly black hair and shiny cheeks he had to shave every other Cinco de Mayo, peering at me doe-eyed from behind his massive desk like a kid playing executive. You wanted to reach over and pat his head and give him a quarter so he could go out and buy himself a Clark Bar. He was so damned cute and cuddly half the women who worked for Great Western felt like bundling him up and taking him home. Some of them *did*, too, and not for milk and cookies. For a fat little guy in his forties, Barney Rivera got laid pretty often—more than ninety percent of the hot-blooded young three-piecers who prowled the singles bars, anyway. I'd known him ten years and it had been that way the whole decade. A legend in his own time, old Barney.

He reached out and scooped up a couple of peppermints from the dish on his desk and popped them into his mouth. Peppermints, yet. Keyes would have lighted a cigar or a pipe; Keyes would have sneered a little and shuffled a few papers and said something wise about the detection of insurance fraud. Peppermints. The whole thing just didn't seem right.

I said, "How long has Ragged-Ass Gulch been a ghost?"

"Most of this century," Barney said. "It flourished for three or four years in the eighteen-fifties; had a population of fifteen hundred at its peak. But then the gold petered out and the miners left for other diggings. There were only a hundred or so people left by eighteen-sixty."

"When did it get renamed Musket Creek?"

"Sometime in the sixties; after the creek that runs through the place. By the turn of the century, only about thirty people were left. Sixteen today, like I said—living up there in virtual isolation."

"Why?"

"Why what?"

"Why do they live there? Gold-hunters?"

"A couple of them, I gather," Barney said. "But that's not important. The one thing they all have in common is that they like living in isolation and want to be left alone; and that's the crux of the problem—they *aren't* being left alone."

"So who's bothering them?"

"A group of developers called the Northern Development Corporation," Barney said, and went on to lay out the full story for me. It went like this:

Musket Creek, née Ragged-Ass Gulch, was some two hundred and fifty miles north of San Francisco, twenty miles from the nearest town of any size, Weaverville, and at the end of seven miles of unpaved road that snaked through the mountains off State Highway 299. The tourists hadn't discovered it because it was so far off the beaten track, but that was all about to change if Northern Development had its way.

Most of the land in the area was government protected—the Shasta–Trinity National Recreation Area—but the land on which Musket Creek sat was owned by Trinity County. The Northern people had begun buying it up during the past year, with the intention of turning Musket Creek into a place the tourists would flock to: widening and paving the access road; restoring the rundown buildings that still stood there, after the fashion of the gaudier Mother Lode towns; adding things like a Frontier Town Amusement Park, stables for horseback rides up into the wilderness, and a couple of lodges to accommodate vacationers and overnight guests.

The Musket Creek residents were up in arms over this. They didn't want to live in a tourist trap and they didn't want to be forced out of their homes by a bunch of outsiders. So they had banded together and hired a law firm to try to block development and further land sales; to get Musket Creek named as a state historical site. Lawsuits were still pending against Northern Development, but the residents were pessimistic; they figured it was just a matter of time before the bulldozers and workmen moved in and another little piece of history died and was reincarnated as a chunk of modern commercialism.

One of them seemed to have been unwilling to accept that fate, however, and had taken matters into his own hands. Four of the town's abandoned buildings had burned to the ground ten days ago, including the remains of a "fandango hall"—a saloon-and-gambling house—that the developers had been particularly interested in restoring. The Northern combine thought it was a blatant case of arson, and had put pressure on the county sheriff's department to investigate; but the law had found no evidence that the fire had been deliberately set, and the official report tabbed it as "of unknown origin."

Bad feelings were running high by this time, on both sides. And they got worse—much worse. Two days ago, there had been another fire, not in Musket Creek this time but in Redding thirty miles away, where Northern Development had its offices. The home of the president of the corporation, a man named Munroe Randall, who had also been the most outspoken against the citizens of Musket Creek, had gone up in flames shortly before midnight. Randall had gone with it. He was not supposed to be home that night—it was common knowledge that he was going to San Francisco on company business—but he'd put off the trip at the last minute. He had evidently been asleep when the blaze started, and was overcome by smoke before he could get out of the burning house. There was no apparent evidence of arson; as far as the local authorities were concerned, his death was accidental.

But Barney Rivera wasn't so sure. What made him skeptical was the fact that Great Western carried a $100,000 double indemnity "key man" policy on Randall's life and on the lives of the two remaining partners, Martin Treacle and Frank O'Daniel. Insurance companies are always skeptical when a heavily insured party dies under unusual circumstances, especially when his business partners are the beneficiaries. Great Western would save $100,000 if Randall's death turned out to be murder instead of an accident; and they would save $200,000 if it was murder and the other two partners had something to do with it. I was here because Great Western was a small company and did not maintain an investigative staff, preferring to farm out that kind of work to private operatives like me. And I had done a fair amount of work for them over the years.

"Questions?" Barney said when he was done explaining.

"Sure. How long has the Northern partnership been in effect?"

"Seven years. They started small, buying up land in the Redding area and building houses on it. That was back during the big real estate boom, so naturally they made a potful. They started purchasing land for the Musket Creek project a little over a year ago."

"Same three partners from the beginning?"

"Yes."

"Equal partners?"

"No. Randall had forty percent; Treacle and O'Daniel split the other sixty."

"Do those two also get Randall's forty percent, now that he's dead?"

"No. But they do get the chance to buy out his share from his estate."

"When did they take out the double indemnity policy?"

"Just after they formed the partnership."

"A point in favor of the two survivors," I said. "Why wait seven years to knock off Randall?"

"Money—what else? They need it, bad. Northern Development isn't doing too well these days. Overextended themselves on land purchases and a housing development near Red Bluff, for one thing. And the Musket Creek lawsuit has been a drain on their capital; they had most of their eggs in that basket. There's a good chance they'll go under if they don't get a break pretty soon."

"A break like a nice fat chunk of insurance money."

"It'd help, that's for sure," Barney said. "Obvious motive. Maybe too obvious."

"Maybe. How did Randall get along with the other two?"

"Fine, according to Stan Zemansky, our company rep in Redding. Stan sold them the policy and he knows the three of them fairly well. No business hassles, no personal feuds—at least none that any of them is talking about."

"What does Zemansky think about Randall's death?"

"Accident, same as everybody else."

"How likely is it one of the Musket Creek citizens set the fire that killed him?"

"Likely enough. The bad feelings between them and Northern Development run deep."

"Groups of people like that usually have a leader," I said. "Who would that be in Musket Creek?"

"Man named Coleclaw, Jack Coleclaw. Runs the local store. Sort of an unofficial mayor. He and Randall had some run-ins, one of them public.

"Violence? Or just words?"

"Just words."

I lapsed into silence. I was thinking that if I took the job, it would mean driving up to Trinity County right away and spending some time in Redding and Musket Creek. Which would put the kibosh on my vacation plans. I didn't like the idea of disappointing Kerry—not only because she had arranged for some time off at the ad agency where she worked, and we had planned a nice quiet ten days together in Santa Barbara, our first real getaway trip in the year we'd known each other; but also because she'd been withdrawn and tired-looking lately. Overwork, she said. I had a feeling there was more to it than that, but she wouldn't talk about it. All she'd say was that she needed to get out of the city for a while and then she'd feel better.

And now this—Ragged-Ass Gulch.

But what could I do? My bank account was not exactly bulging, and Great Western paid well for services rendered and allowed a generous expense sheet. If it were any other time I might have been able to let Eberhardt handle it; but he was already working on a missing-person thing for a well-to-do local family, one of those cases where a rich kid goes off to find the meaning of life, drops out of sight, and usually turns up in a commune or maybe soliciting funds for somebody's screwball religion. Eberhardt had turned up the job himself, the first major piece of business he'd brought into the agency since I'd taken him on as a partner six months ago. Even if it hadn't been lucrative work, which it was, I could not very well ask him to drop it and rush up to Trinity County just so I could be free to spend some time in the sun with my lady friend. . . .

A sharp rapping noise made me blink: Barney was using his knuckles on the desktop. "Hey," he said, "you still home in there? Or did part of you go out to lunch?"

I gave him a crooked grin. "I'm still here. Just mentally bemoaning my lot in life. All right, Barney. I'll get to work right away. Usual rates?"

"Yup. You going to pad the expense sheet this time?"

"Hell no. I never padded an expense sheet in my life and you know it."

"Yeah," he said, "and it bothers me. You're too god-damned honest. Couldn't you at least stick on a couple of beers that you didn't have? Or an extra dime for the parking meter? It'd restore my faith in the fundamental immorality of mankind."

"I'll see what I can do."

"Try real hard," he said. "I wouldn't feel comfortable working with a saint."

In spite of myself the word "saint" made me think of Jeanne Emerson, a very attractive Chinese photojournalist who had developed an idealized view of me and my job—a sin-eater, she'd called me, only half-jokingly. But that had all been before the night a couple of months ago when I'd finally let her come over to my flat to take some photographs for an article on me she was planning to do. I hadn't wanted to be alone with her, because it had become obvious that her interest in me wasn't strictly professional, and I happened to be in love with Kerry; I'd been stalling Jeanne for weeks. But then I'd given in in a weak moment, and Jeanne had come over, and what had happened after that . . .

"Hey," Barney said again, "now what? You look constipated all of a sudden."

I stopped thinking. That had always been one of my problems: I thought too damned much about nearly everything. "Only one of us is full of crap, my friend," I said, "and that's you. Let's have the file."

He gave it to me, grinning, and I thumbed through it. Lists of names, addresses, personal and background data on the three Northern partners, copies of the Redding police report on Munroe Randall's death and the Trinity County Sheriff's Department report on their Musket Creek investigation, other pertinent information—most of it on computer printout sheets. The address of Stan Zemansky's insurance agency was there too. I tucked the file into the calfskin briefcase Kerry had bought me for Christmas—to upgrade my image a little, she'd said—and then got on my feet.

Barney stood too, speared another peppermint, and came around his desk. He looked me up and down and shook his head admiringly.

"Got to admit it," he said. "You're looking good."

"You admitted it when I came in, remember?"

"How much weight have you lost, anyhow?"

"A little over twenty pounds."

"How long did it take you?"

"Three months, about."

"What'd you do, just give up eating?"

"More or less. Plenty of salad and eggs."

He pulled a face. "I hate salad and eggs."

"Me too."

"Took a lot of willpower, huh?"

"Yeah. I slipped a couple of times at first, but after a while it wasn't too bad."

"So everybody keeps telling me," Barney said. He patted his ample midriff. "But I can't seem to do it myself. I like food too much. *Carne asada*—that's my main weakness. Did I ever take you to my cousin Carlos's place in the Mission? No? You never tasted *carne asada* the way he makes it. A gallon of sour cream, and those sweet onions he uses . . . ah Jesus."

"I think I better pass."

"Willpower," he said. "I wish I had it." He gave me another examining look. "Yeah, you look great. Except—"

"Except what?"

He snickered. "Just what *is* that thing on your upper lip?"

I reached up and touched it; I couldn't seem to break myself of the habit of doing that every time somebody called attention to it. "It's a mustache," I said. "What did you think it was?"

"It looks like a hooker's false eyelash stuck on there."

"Ha ha. Very funny."

"Kind of scraggly, isn't it? Or did you just start growing it?"

"I've had it for a month," I said defensively. "It looks all right to *me*. What's wrong with it?"

"Nothing a razor won't fix. How come you grew a mustache at your age?"

"What am I, a candidate for the old folks' home?" I could feel myself getting a little miffed. Which was stupid, because Barney was only having some fun with me; but I had taken a lot of ribbing about the mustache in the past month, principally from Eberhardt and

Kerry, and I'd had enough. If it hadn't been for all the ribbing, in fact, I might have shaved the thing off by now. As matters stood, each new crack only made me more determined to keep it. "So I grew a mustache," I said. "So what's the big deal?"

"Why?" he said.

"Why what?"

"Why did you grow it? To impress your lady?"

"No."

"You figured it'd make you look younger?"

"No."

"Because of all the weight you lost?"

"No! I grew it because I felt like it."

"Okay, okay. Kind of touchy on the subject, aren't you."

"No, damn it, I'm not touchy on the goddamn subject!"

Barney grinned. "I still think it looks like a hooker's false eyelash," he said.

I suggested a fun thing he could do with himself, caught up my briefcase, told him I'd be in touch, and went out stroking the damn mustache like it was a pet caterpillar. By the time I realized what I was doing, I was halfway across the anteroom. And Barney, the little bastard, was having himself a noisy chuckle behind his closed office door.

TWO

The office I shared with Eberhardt was a small, converted third-floor loft in a building on O'Farrell Street, a hop and a skip from Van Ness Avenue's automobile row. The building was owned by an unconverted slum landlord named Crawford, who looked like a Tammany Hall politician and had the soul and heart of a pirate; he was charging us eight hundred dollars a month for the place, an outrageous price but one that was not far out of line with what other office space was going for in the city these days. San Francisco was full of pirates, it seemed. Pretty soon they would drive everybody else out to the suburbs and then they could start raping and pillaging each other, as the old Caribbean buccaneers used to do in places like Tortuga. It was a thought to keep you warm when the rent came due, anyway.

The door was locked when I got there. When I let myself in the first thing I saw was the light fixture hanging from the ceiling. It looked like nothing so much as an upside-down grappling hook surrounded by clusters of brass testicles. It was the ugliest light fixture I had ever seen and I hated it and I kept threatening to tear it down one of these days, landlord or no landlord. But I never seemed to get around to doing it. Maybe there was something psychological in that; maybe subconsciously I needed to keep it around in order to have something to take out my nonviolent aggressions on. Or maybe, somewhere down at the bottom of my warped old psyche, I considered the thing to be a fitting symbol of my life and work. Who the hell knew?

I switched it on, leered at it, and went over to my desk. The rest of the office wasn't such-a-much, either. It was about twenty feet square, and it had beige walls, a beige carpet that we'd recently put down to cover bare wood and paint-stained linoleum, a skylight that a former tenant had cut into the ceiling, three windows and two views—one view of the back end of the Federal Building, the other of a blank brick wall—and that was all it had other than Eberhardt's and my office equipment. If you needed to use the john, you had to go downstairs to the Slim-Taper Shirt Company, "The Slim-Taper Look is the Right Look," and hop around on one foot until one of their employees unlocked the toilet *they* had.

There weren't any calls on my answering machine, nor were there any scrawled messages from Eberhardt on my desk, as there sometimes were. Which meant he probably hadn't come in at all today. I remembered his telling me he might have to go to Stinson Beach to check a lead on his missing rich girl.

I sat down and looked at the telephone and thought about calling Kerry at the Bates and Carpenter ad agency. But I didn't do it. Telling her the Santa Barbara vacation would have to be postponed was something best done in person. Tonight I would tell her, when we had dinner. Dinner was all we'd have together tonight, once she heard, but then life is full of disappointments and frustrations. Life, to coin a lyrical phrase, sometimes sucks.

So I got out the *Northern Development vs. Ragged-Ass Gulch* file Barney Rivera had given me and read through it. About the only things I learned were some sketchy background details on the three partners.

Munroe Randall. Forty-four at the time of his death. Native of Kansas. M.B.A. from some college I'd never heard of in the Midwest; lived in California for eighteen years, in Redding for thirteen. Unmarried. Worked for two large real estate firms in the Redding area before founding Northern Development with his own capital supplemented by cash from the other two partners and bank loans. Excellent credit rating. Numerous personal references.

Frank O'Daniel. Thirty-nine. Born in Idaho, had lived in Redding since his early teens. B.B.A. degree in Accounting from Chico State; he was the company's pencil pusher and paper shuffler. Worked as a CPA before throwing in with Randall. Married, wife's name Helen, no children. Credit rating somewhat shaky: he or his wife or both of them liked to spend money even when they were on the shorts. Personal references good.

Martin Treacle. Forty-one. Native of Red Bluff, a few miles south of Redding. Limited college education: a year and a half at a Humboldt County Junior College. Holder of various sales jobs in the Redding/Red Bluff area, all with established firms, at increasingly larger salaries. Similar position with Northern Development—the company's glad-hander and silver-tongue. Divorced five years, one daughter; ex-wife and the daughter now living in San Diego. Credit rating better than O'Daniel's but not quite as high as Randall's. Personal references good.

I had just put down the data sheet on Treacle when the door opened and I had a visitor. And the visitor, it turned out, was Martin Treacle himself.

He came in a little diffidently, poking his head around the door edge first, as if he thought something peculiar might be going on in here. They get ideas like that from bad books and bad TV programs—all the distorted portrayals of the allegedly weird, violent, and alcoholic world of private eyes. It is to laugh. Anyhow, he came all the way in when he saw I was alone and relatively harmless-looking—no gat or top-heavy blonde or quart of Old Panther Piss in sight—and announced who he was and what he wanted. Which was to offer me his and Frank O'Daniel's full cooperation in my inquiry into the death of Munroe Randall.

I studied him for a time. He was a handsome guy, lean and fit, with close-cropped black hair and a mustache that was fuller and shapelier than mine and definitely did not look like a hooker's false eyelash. He wore a dark-blue gabardine suit, nice but not high-priced, with accessories in the same class. He seemed very earnest about everything he said, and there was a kind of hopeful glint in his eyes, as if he wanted very much to make a good impression on me. A salesman, all right. But I decided to give him the benefit of the doubt, for the time being at least, and assume that he had come here in good faith and that his offer was guileless as well as genuine.

I said, "How did you get my name, Mr. Treacle?"

"A Mr. Rivera at Great Western Insurance gave it to me. I talked to him not more than half an hour ago."

"Is that why you came down from Redding? To talk to Great Western's investigators?"

"No, I was here on other business. But I thought it would be a good idea to stay on top of things while I'm in the city."

"Mm."

"Frank and I welcome the investigation, we want you to know that. We have nothing to hide."

"I'm glad to hear it."

"Yes. The sooner Great Western is satisfied," he said, "the sooner Frank and I collect on our policy. As we're entitled to. So naturally we want to cooperate to the fullest."

"Naturally. Is that all you're interested in?"

"Pardon me?"

"Don't either of you care about what happened to Randall? If he was murdered, don't you want to see whoever killed him caught and punished?"

"Well, of course," Treacle said. "That goes without saying."

"Even if it costs you the extra hundred thousand double indemnity?"

"Of course. But Frank and I are both convinced that the Redding police are right—Munroe's death was a tragic accident. It couldn't have been anything else."

"Perhaps not. Were you and Randall friends as well as business partners?"

"Good friends, yes."

"You don't seem very upset about his death."

"It came as quite a shock, believe me."

"But without any lingering grief."

"I'm not the grieving sort," Treacle said earnestly. "No, I'm a realist. People live, people die, life goes on."

A philosopher too, I thought. Aristotle Treacle, the compassionate one. I said, "And you just want what's yours while it does, right?"

"Well, I wouldn't put it that way. The fact of the matter is, it's not Frank and me who need the insurance money—not personally. It's the company. You may already know this, but we're not in a stable financial position at present. Haven't been for some months. And Munroe's death hasn't helped matters at all, obviously."

I asked him, "How did your company get into this financial bind?" to see if his answer would jibe with what Barney Rivera had told me.

It did. "Frankly," he said, "we've made some ill-advised purchases and investments over the past couple of years. We'd be all right if our Musket Creek development package had opened up as planned, but that didn't happen thanks to the people of Musket Creek and their lawyers. You know about the litigation, of course?"

"I've been filled in."

"Well," he said, and shrugged, and smiled at me in his hopeful way.

I looked at him some more in silence. I kept trying to dislike him—he was glib, he was materialistic, he didn't seem to have much of an interior; he was everything that annoyed me in salesmen and the modern business executive—and yet he was so damned *earnest* that I couldn't work up much of an antipathy toward him. Maybe if it turned out he was implicated in Munroe Randall's death, or that he was *some* kind of crook, I could start detesting him. Right now I would have to settle for being mildly aggrieved at his existence.

I said, "About your partner's death," and he paused in the process of unwrapping a long, thin panatela that he'd taken from his inside jacket pocket. "With all the bad blood between the Musket Creek citizens and your company, murder's not out of the question. Or would you say otherwise?"

"Well . . . the police seemed sure that the fire was accidental. . . ."

"Still," I said, pushing him a little, "it *could* be murder."

He clipped off the end of his cigar, put the end and the crumpled cellophane carefully into my wastebasket, and used a thin silver lighter to fire up. He didn't say anything.

So I pushed a little more. "You must know those people in Musket Creek. Did any of them hate Munroe Randall enough to want him dead?"

"They all hated Munroe," Treacle said with some bitterness. "And Frank and me too."

"Are any of them capable of murder, in your opinion?"

"They're probably all capable of it. They're all loonies, you know."

"How do you mean that, Mr. Treacle?"

"Strange people—very strange. Clannish, totally withdrawn from the mainstream of society and totally against progressive thinking of any kind."

It sounded like a set speech, the kind to be delivered to lawyers and judges. I said, "I don't see that that makes them loonies."

"Believe me, they are. One of them even threatened *me* a few weeks ago."

"Is that so? Which one?"

"A man named Robideaux. An artist—a bad artist, judging from the examples of his work I've seen."

"What were the circumstances of the threat?"

"I was out inspecting one of our Musket Creek parcels. Robideaux came by and started in with the usual nonsense—"

"What nonsense is that?"

"Environmentalist nonsense. Desecration of wilderness land, the evils of free enterprise—that sort of crap."

I had nothing to say to that.

"Well, I ignored him," Treacle said. "I wasn't about to be drawn into a pointless argument. That made him even angrier and he said I'd better watch myself around there because someday somebody might decide to shoot at me."

"Nobody ever did, I take it."

"I haven't been back since."

"Did Robideaux or anyone else from Musket Creek ever threaten Munroe Randall?"

"Not that I know about."

"I understand he had a public argument with a man named Coleclaw. No threats then?"

"No. It was a shouting match at our attorney's office; he was taking depositions from Coleclaw and some of the others from out there. Coleclaw called Munroe a liar and a thief, and a few other things, but he didn't make any threats."

"How about Frank O'Daniel? Has *he* been threatened?"

"No. He'd have told me."

The smoke from Treacle's cigar was aggravating both my lungs and my sinuses; I used my hand to shred a thick plume of it. I never did like cigars much—or the men who smoke them in somebody else's office without asking permission. More ammunition for my campaign to dislike Martin Treacle.

I said, "I'd appreciate it if you'd put that out, Mr. Treacle," because I'd had enough and I didn't feel like being tolerant any more.

"Out?" he said blankly.

"Your cigar. The smoke is bothering me."

He looked at the panatela in a surprised way, looked at me again, and said, "Oh. I'm sorry, I didn't realize . . ." Then he looked around the office, probably for an ashtray. There wasn't one in sight. I keep one in my bottom desk drawer, but I decided I didn't feel like obliging him with it. So I sat there, waiting, and he looked at me again, a little helplessly this time, hesitated, and then got up trailing smoke and went over to the window that looked out on the blank brick wall next door. He tugged at the sash, couldn't open it, gave me another helpless glance, tugged again, and finally got it to slide up. He threw the cigar out into the airshaft, without looking to see what was down below—not that there was anything flammable down there or I would have said something about it and stopped him. Then he shut the window and dusted his hands and came back to his chair and said, "I'm sorry," in a nonplussed sort of way. But he didn't sit down again. Instead he shot the sleeve of his suit coat and glanced at his watch.

"I should be going," he said. "I've got a four o'clock appointment. But if you have more questions . . ."

"Not right now."

"Well then," he said, but he wasn't quite ready to leave yet. "When will you be going to Redding?"

"Tomorrow, probably."

"You'll want to talk to Frank right away, I imagine."

"Among others."

"I'll call him tonight and let him know you're coming. Is there anything you'll need, any arrangements he can make for you?"

"Just a list of the Musket Creek residents," I said. "Plus a little background on each one, if possible."

"No problem. I'll tell Miss Irwin to work up something for you."

"Who's Miss Irwin?"

"Shirley Irwin, our secretary." He looked at his watch again. "Well," he said. Then he paused, looking at me as if he expected me to get up and shake his hand and tell him how much I appreciated his cooperation. I stayed where I was, shaking hands with myself. He said, "Well," another time, and followed it with, "I'll be going then. I should be back in Redding myself the day after tomorrow. I expect we'll see each other again soon."

"I expect we will, Mr. Treacle," I said.

He nodded and smiled—earnest and hopeful all the way—and turned for the door. Before he got there, though, it opened and Eberhardt came in looking grumpy. Eb ran into him, and Treacle reacted by hopping awkwardly out of the way like a ruptured jackrabbit. They looked at each other for a couple of seconds. After which Treacle said, "Excuse me, I'm sorry," and beat it out through the door.

Eberhardt said to me, "What was that?"

"Martin Treacle. Real estate developer from Redding."

"Yeah? Him?"

"Minor-league," I said.

"Client?"

"No. One of the objects of a new case."

"That's good. Or is it?"

"I'm not sure yet. Could be."

"Don't tell me about it yet," he said. "I got to sit down first and unwind."

"Unwind from what?"

"That goddamn drive over to Stinson Beach. I hate that goddamn drive. That road scares me to death."

I nodded sympathetically. The road scared me to death, too. It wound along the cliffsides for miles of sheer-sided dropoffs to rocks and ocean, and it wasn't in very good repair.

Eberhardt sat down, put his feet up on his desk, and rubbed the scar behind his ear. The scar was from one of the bullets a gunman had pumped into him last August, putting him into a coma for seventeen days; the same gunman had pumped a bullet into me, too, and laid me up in the hospital for a while, and gave me a bad left arm that didn't quite work the way it used to. The shooting was also the direct reason—there were several indirect ones—for his taking an early retirement from the San Francisco cops. Things had been bad for him for a while after that, until I gave in out of friendship and a smattering of pity and took him into my agency as a full partner. The partnership had worked out much better than I'd imagined it would. Eb was happy, I was happy, neither of us was starving to death as a result of having to split the profits, and that pirate Sam Crawford was getting his blood booty right on time the first of every month. Everything was just dandy—knock wood.

He sighed and ran a hand over the angles and blunt planes of his face. He was a year younger than my fifty-four and looked his age. Kerry said I didn't look *my* age now that I'd taken off weight; but she also said the mustache made me look like Brian Keith trying to play Groucho Marx. Kerry has an acid wit sometimes. An off-the-wall wit, too: half the things she thinks are funny I don't even understand.

"Better," Eb said, pretty soon. "It's been a hell of a day."

"You find your missing heiress?"

"Not yet, but I'm getting close. I found a girlfriend of hers out there at Stinson Beach; the girlfriend lives with a guy who collects driftwood and has hair down to his ass and they put Trudy up for a few days last week. She left on Saturday to go to a retreat up in the Napa Valley."

"What kind of retreat?"

"What kind you think? It's called the Temple of Good Karma and Inner Peace, and it's run by a guru named Mahatma something-or-other—not Gandhi. He's probably got hair down to *his* ass too."

"Your prejudices are showing, Eb."

''Prejudices? Hell, I got nothing against guys with long hair. I got nothing against good karma or inner peace or gurus, either—unless the whole thing's a scam to bilk money out of rich kids like Trudy Bigelow, which it usually is.''

''I guess. So you've pretty much got things wrapped up, then?''

''Maybe. Depends on whether or not she's still at the retreat; I'll go up tomorrow and see. If she is I'll have to call her old man to find out how he wants to handle it.''

''Yeah.''

''What's the matter? You sound disappointed.''

''Well, I was hoping maybe you could take over this case up in Trinity County. On account of my vacation. But I guess that idea's out.''

''It is if your case is a hot one.''

''In more ways than one.'' I gave him a brief rundown. ''So it can't be put off,'' I said. ''I'll have to leave right away. Kerry's not going to like postponing the vacation—she's been looking forward to Santa Barbara.''

''Why not take her with you?''

''What?''

''Take her along to Trinity County,'' he said. ''Nice country up there—Mount Shasta, Shasta Lake, the McCloud River. Good fishing too.''

''Hell, Eb, I can't do that . . .''

''Why not?''

''Mixing business and pleasure never works out. What's she going to do while I'm working?''

''Same things you were planning to do in Santa Barbara.''

''Not hardly. We were going to rent a cabin cruiser down there, go out to the Channel Islands. She likes boats; she and her ex-husband used to own one in Santa Monica.''

''They got boats at Shasta Lake,'' Eberhardt said. ''It's not the ocean and there aren't any real islands, but it's pretty nice anyway. An investigation like this, you should have it in the bag in two or three days. That still gives you a week or so to rent a boat, go up one of the finger lakes and fish and drink beer. Sounds good to me.''

Well, it sounded good to me too, now that I thought about it. But I said, ''I dunno, Eb. She probably wouldn't go for it.''

"You don't understand women worth a damn, do you? She'll go for it. Just ask her."

"Okay, I'll ask her," I said. "But I still don't think she'll like the idea."

"Of course I'll come with you," Kerry said at dinner that night. "I've never been to Shasta Lake."

"You're sure you don't mind? I mean, the job and the last-minute switch in plans . . ."

"I understand about business," she said. "Don't you think I understand about things like that?"

"Sure, but—"

"I understand," she said. "I'm a very understanding person. We'll go up to Trinity County, I'll sit around and wait while you do your work, and if there's any time left we'll rent a boat and go fishing or whatever. We'll have a gay old time. Now let's not talk about it any more."

I looked at her. Then I sighed inwardly and thought: Give me strength, Lord. It's going to be a long ten days.

THREE

The drive to Redding takes about four hours. We left at eight o'clock on Friday morning and got up there a little past noon.

Redding is the jumping-off point for the Shasta–Trinity National Forest, Shasta Lake and Shasta Dam, and a number of other wilderness and recreation areas in the far northern part of the state. It has a population of around forty thousand, the upper reaches of the Sacramento River runs through it, and so does a main line of the Southern Pacific railroad; and that's pretty much all you can say about it. A nice enough little city, but without any real distinctive qualities—a place you might decide to live in but that you probably wouldn't care to visit unless you were on your way someplace else. At least that was how this reluctant visitor felt as I took the downtown exit off

Highway 5 and drove across the narrow squiggle of the river. But then, I wasn't in a particularly charitable mood at the moment.

I said to Kerry, "I guess the first thing we should do is find a motel."

"Uh-huh," she said.

"Unless you want to stop and get something to eat."

"No, I'm not hungry."

"Any preferences for the motel? You can check the Triple-A guide . . ."

"No. Whatever you want."

That was the way it had been all the way up—four hours of monosyllables and simple declarative sentences. Every time I looked at her, and she caught me at it, she would smile and give me eye contact for a couple of seconds; but then I'd glance at her a few seconds later, and she'd be wearing a blank expression and staring off into space. Something was troubling her, all right. And it wasn't just the fact that I'd taken on this job, or the switch in vacation plans; Kerry was not the type to pout over things like that. A couple of times I'd asked her what was wrong. But she'd said nothing was wrong, and when I pressed her she'd gotten a little snippy, the way women do when they don't feel like communicating. It was starting to worry me. She was shutting me out and I couldn't seem to find a way to reach her when she did that. Whatever was bothering her, I wouldn't get it out of her until she was good and ready to let go of it.

I looked at her again now. That same blank expression and remote stare. The sun slanting in through the windshield gave her auburn hair a fiery cast; her eyes, dark green most of the time, although they seemed to change color according to the fluctuations of her mood, were almost black now. She sat stiff-backed, with her hands folded just under her breasts—a posture that was oddly mannequin-like, as if you could reach over and take her limbs and rearrange them into different positions with no resistance at all.

My throat closed up a little. Something stirred through me, like little puffs of wind among dry leaves. God, how I loved that woman. . . .

I found a motel on North Market Street downtown, the Sportsman's Rest, that had some shade trees and a big swimming pool. The room we were given was nice enough, except that everything was either bolted or nailed down, including a painting of some dubious-looking fruit that nobody in his right mind would want to steal. It was stuffy in there—the temperature was in the high seventies, unseasonably hot for early May—and after I brought in the bags I went and switched on the air conditioner. Kerry hadn't said a word since we'd pulled in; and when I asked her if she planned to go swimming, all I got in response was "Maybe." I decided the thing for me to do was to go away and let her be alone for a while. And that was what I did.

My first stop was the Redding police station. It was only a few blocks away, and the woman in the motel office had given me a city map and directions after I'd checked in. The officer in charge of the Munroe Randall investigation was a sergeant named Betters, who turned out to be a pleasant and cooperative sort. But he didn't have much to tell me beyond what was in his report.

He and his men had twice sifted through the burned-out remains of the Randall house, without turning up any evidence that suggested arson as the source of the blaze. Nor had the coroner's post-mortem contributed anything of a suspicious nature. Randall had evidently died of smoke inhalation while trying to escape the burning house; firefighters had found his body sprawled in an areaway leading to the back door. Aside from the fire itself, none of the neighbors had seen or heard anything out of the ordinary that night. One of them, who'd known Randall pretty well, stated that he had kept paint thinner and other combustible materials inside the attached garage; and as near as Betters had been able to determine, the garage had been the fire's point of origin. The official verdict was spontaneous combustion and accidental death.

"There's no way at all it could have been arson?" I asked him.

"Well, it *could* have been, sure," Betters said. "You can never be a hundred percent certain in cases like this. But if it was, then the torch is either a topflight professional or a blind-lucky amateur."

"I take it nobody connected with Randall had anything fire-related in his background?"

"No, nobody. At least not as far as we could determine."

"Does that include the citizens of Musket Creek?"

"It does. The county sheriff's men ran checks on the Musket Creek residents, went out and talked to a few of them; they all seemed glad to hear that Randall was dead, but you can't arrest somebody for that."

"Treacle and O'Daniel checked out clean too?"

"Solid citizens, both of them."

"And Northern Development? No hint of anything going on behind the scenes?"

"None."

"Okay," I said, "I guess that's about it for now. But I would like to take a look at what's left of the Randall home."

"Sure thing. Cleanup hasn't started yet; it's all just sitting there waiting."

"Fenced off or anything like that?"

He shook his head. "You can walk right in."

I asked him how to get there, and he told me, and I went off to have my look. Randall had lived in a wooded development off Churn Creek Road, east of Highway 5 and five miles or so from downtown Redding. I found the street without too much trouble, and the remains immediately: the place was like a huge black scar on the otherwise serene and affluent face of the neighborhood.

The houses were in the six-figure class, all fairly new, some on two- or three-acre parcels. Randall's had been one of the smaller places, built on maybe an acre of land, with a line of spruce separating it from the neighbor on one side and a redwood-stake fence forming the boundary on the other. There wasn't much left of it. Fire had gutted both the house and the attached garage, collapsing all but one wall of the house and a blackened brick column that had once been the fireplace chimney. Most of the rear wall had toppled outward, so that a jumbled fan of charred wood and brick lay over a flagstone terrace, a rectangle of lawn, and a kidney-shaped swimming pool; nobody had bothered to drain the pool and debris floated in it like bones in a black soup. It had been some hot fire, all right. Part of the boundary fence and some of the trees were heavily scorched, and the singed corpse of a fruit tree stood out front like an ugly monument to death.

Wearing an old trenchcoat I'd brought along to protect my clothes from soot, I wandered among the debris and used a stick to poke around here and there. It had all been sifted through pretty thoroughly, as Betters had assured me. I hadn't expected to find anything, and I didn't. But you never know. It's easy enough to overlook something in the remains of a fire like this one.

I gave it up after a while, took off the trenchcoat and stowed it back in the trunk of my car, and went to cover more old territory: Randall's neighbors. None of them had much to tell me, either—nothing at all that differed from what they'd told Betters and his men. One middle-aged woman, who lived diagonally across the street, allowed as how she had seen a yellow sports car parked just down from Randall's property around 9:00 P.M. on the night of the fire; but when she'd looked again later, it was gone. I took that for what it was worth: little or nothing, probably.

It was after three when I finished canvassing the neighbors. Time for a couple more stops, at least. According to my map, the street on which Stan Zemansky, the insurance agent, had his office was fairly close by; so I went and hunted it up. I was saving Frank O'Daniel for my last stop, because I wanted to be armed with as much information as possible before I interviewed him.

Zemansky was in and "eager to talk to me," meaning Barney Rivera had contacted him and given him instructions to cooperate. He was one of these guys who seem to have been turned out on an assembly line, and who ought to have been sent out into the world wearing a sign that said BATTERIES NOT INCLUDED. He was about forty, had a nice smile and a friendly manner, and an office that said he was selling a lot of insurance; but you took one look at him and you knew he had never had an original thought in his life. He was a product of the times: you programmed him to perform a useful societal function, wound him up and let him go, and he did exactly what he was supposed to and exactly what he was told to by everybody from the politicians on down to his wife. This was what was left of the American middle class: the manufactured and manipulated man. Batteries not included.

"Terrible tragedy, Munroe's death," he said, with the proper amount of gravity in his voice. "He was a prince, he really was. You'd have liked him; everybody did."

"Except the people in Musket Creek," I said.

"Well, they're an odd bunch. Misfits. I mean, you can't stop the tide of progress, can you?"

"Might be better if you could, sometimes."

He gave me a blank look. That kind of comment just did not compute for him.

I asked him if Randall had any personal problems that he knew about, and he said, "Munroe? Heck no. Life was his oyster. And the ladies . . . well, he was a swordsman if I ever knew one. Guy who got as much as Munroe did, how could he have problems?"

"Was there any particular woman in his life?"

"No sir. Like I said, Munroe played the field. A real swordsman."

"His most recent girlfriend, then. Would you know who she was?"

"Well . . . that'd be Penny Belson, I guess. I'm not sure, though. He traded them in pretty fast."

"Uh-huh. Where can I find Penny Belson?"

"She owns a beauty parlor in the downtown mall," Zemansky said. "Fancy place, high-priced; my wife goes there sometimes when she thinks we can afford it. Penny's for Beauty, it's called. Which is kind of ironic. Because it's such a high-priced place, I mean."

I asked him if he thought Randall's death was an accident, and he said, "Definitely. Couldn't be anything else. I mean, that's what the police decided, isn't it?"

I asked him about Martin Treacle and Frank O'Daniel, and he said, "Princes, both of them. I play golf with Frank; I'm just a duffer, you know, but Frank, he shoots in the eighties. He had back-to-back birdies the last time we were out on the old links."

I gave it up finally, thanked him for his time, let him pump my hand another time, and got out of there. The Stan Zemanskys of the world made me feel as if I were either very bright and very sane, or edging my way toward a private room in a twitch bin. Not that it mattered much; I liked my perceptions a hell of a lot better than theirs, either way.

"Life was his oyster," he'd said. "Out on the old links," he'd said. Jesus Christ!

FOUR

From the outside, Penny's for Beauty didn't look like much—just another storefront, except that its front window was curtained instead of open for display, in the middle of an attractive new downtown mall that covered several blocks. But the reception room inside was pretty ritzy: walls painted in cool blues and greens, lots of potted plants and latticework and white wrought-iron furniture. There were half a dozen women in it, five occupying various pieces of wrought-iron and the sixth ensconced behind a reception table with a telephone and an appointment book on it.

All of the women looked at me when I came in. I felt like an idiot standing there under their scrutiny; I always felt like an idiot in places like this, the more or less exclusive domain of women. I also felt myself grinning fatuously at the six females, none of whom grinned back. The smells of shampoo and other beauty salon concoctions were in the air, a mixture that was vaguely reminiscent of disinfectant; it made my nose twitch and I wanted to sneeze. I got that under control, wiped off the stupid grin, and went over to the reception desk.

The woman behind it was a well-groomed blonde, dressed in an outfit that matched the blue-and-green color scheme; she was about forty and made up to look thirty, and you were supposed to believe that her secret was in the various bottles and tubes and decanters on the display shelves at her back, and in whatever was going on—buzzings, clickings, murmurings—beyond a lattice-bordered archway to one side. She gave me the same kind of look a bum might get if he wandered in off the street for a handout, and asked, snootily, if there was anything she could do for me.

I wasn't in a mood to tolerate being sneered at, so I leaned over in front of her and said, "I'm a detective, here to see Penny Belson," in a tough-guy voice. "If she's in, sister, trot her out here so we can talk. Pronto." Philip Marlowe, circa 1940.

But the blonde wasn't a Chandler fan; she blinked at me a couple of times, gnawed her underlip a couple of times, asked my name in a much more polite tone, and then used her telephone to talk to somebody I assumed was Penny Belson. When she put the receiver down she said, "Miss Belson will be right out." Then she sat stiff-backed and stared at me.

The waiting customers were staring at me too; they'd overheard my exchange with the receptionist. But the stares were of a different kind now and I felt better about the whole thing. I put on a little more tough-guy for them, in the form of a glower, and it would have worked out fine if the damned salon smell hadn't been so strong in there. I sneezed right in the middle of the glower, none too quietly, and scared hell out of them and me both.

Another blonde came through the latticed archway, this one about the same age as the receptionist and just as attractive and well-groomed. But she had more poise, a kind of icy self-possession; and her eyes were an odd, striking gray accented by makeup. A very sexy number, if you like them chipped and chiseled and sharp around the eyes and mouth. She was wearing a sort of tailored smock in the same colors as the reception room and the receptionist. She was also wearing an expression as unrevealing as a snowfield in a blizzard. I wouldn't have liked to play poker with her. Or anything else with her, for that matter.

She looked at me and said, "I'm Penny Belson. Come with me, please." That was all; no fuss of any kind. It was in deference to the customers, no doubt—never make a scene in front of customers—but she handled it with aplomb.

So I went through the arch into another room full of women, this batch evidently being tortured in various ways. Most of them were sitting under big hair dryers that looked like hunched, helmeted aliens devouring their heads; a few of these were reading magazines like *Vogue*, a few were having their nails done by manicurists, and a few were either asleep or dead. None of them paid any attention to me as I followed Penny Belson on a course to another door at the far end.

This one led to La Belson's private office, a room in marked contrast to the other two. Flat white decor, a mostly bare desk, some file cabinets, three chairs, a bowl of cut flowers on a small side table, and a still life on one wall. Sterile. No frills, no nonsense. A room where business was transacted and the take was counted assiduously at the end of each day.

She shut the door, went to the desk, sat down behind it, waited for me to take a chair uninvited, and said, "Now then. You're with the Redding police?"

"No, ma'am."

"The county sheriff's department?"

"No. Actually, I'm a private investigator."

That got me a flat, contemplative look. "You told Miss Adley that you were a policeman," she said.

"No, ma'am. I told her I was a detective and that's what I am."

"I see." She smiled faintly and wryly, without humor. "I suppose you're here about Munroe Randall."

"Yes. I'm working for his insurance company." I had my wallet out, for the purpose of showing her my ID, but she made a dismissive gesture. I put the wallet away again.

"You're wasting your time and mine," she said. "I can't tell you anything about his death. As I've already explained to the police, I hadn't seen him for over a month before he died."

"Oh? Why is that, Miss Belson?"

"If you'd known Munroe, you wouldn't have to ask that question. He liked women—lots of different women. He got bored very easily."

"Does that mean he'd broken off your relationship?"

"That's what it means."

"Suddenly?"

"Very. But I wasn't surprised."

"Were you upset?"

"Not particularly."

"Meaning you no longer cared for him either?"

"Meaning I also get bored easily."

Uh-huh, I thought. I said, "Do you know who he began seeing after he ended things with you?"

"Who he began seeing *before* he ended things with me, you mean."

"Do you know the woman's name?"

"I didn't at the time," she said.

"But you do now?"

She hesitated. Then she said, "A beauty parlor is a great place for gossip. You'd be amazed at the things a person can find out here."

"I can imagine."

"No you can't. Not really. The damnedest secrets come out, no matter how well hidden they're intended to be."

"Was Randall's new affair a secret?"

"Yes. A big one."

"Why?"

Again she hesitated, as if weighing things in her mind. One shoulder lifted and fell in a delicate shrug and she said, "He made a mistake. He decided to start playing in his own backyard."

"I'm not sure I understand that, Miss Belson."

"You're a detective. You ought to be able to figure it out."

"A married woman? The wife of someone he knew?"

She didn't say anything. But there was a malicious little glint in her eyes.

"The wife of one of his business partners?" I asked.

"Only one of his business partners is married," she said.

"Frank O'Daniel's wife?"

"Little Helen," La Belson said. The malice was in her voice now.

"You know her, then?"

"Helen? Oh yes, she used to be one of my customers."

"Used to be?"

"She decided to try another salon in town. About six weeks ago, as a matter of fact."

"Because she'd started an affair with Randall?"

The delicate shrug again. "Why don't you ask her?"

Cute stuff—playing games, telling me what I wanted to know without actually saying it. Maybe. It could be a lie, too; for all I knew she had something against Helen O'Daniel and wanted to do her dirt. That might explain the coyness: if she didn't come right out and accuse Mrs. O'Daniel of anything illicit, she couldn't get herself sued for slander.

On the other hand, it might be the truth. Not that an affair between Randall and Mrs. O'Daniel had to mean anything sinister. I just didn't know enough yet about the principals involved to form much of an opinion either way.

I tried prying more information out of La Belson, but she wasn't about to give me more than she already had. I asked her a few other questions, also without finding out anything new, and got up to leave.

She said, "All these questions—you don't honestly believe Munroe's death was anything but an accident, do you?"

"I've got an open mind. What's your opinion, Miss Belson?"

"Munroe was a careless man. With women, with everything else in his life. Including flammable materials around his house." Another shrug. "Accidents happen," she said.

"So do murders," I said.

I left her and managed to run the gauntlet of hair dryers and fat women without disgracing myself. Along with the receptionist, Miss Adley, there were only two customers waiting out front now. I went straight on out, minding my own business, and just as I was shutting the door behind me I heard Miss Adley say in a stage whisper, "Cops. They're all assholes."

Penny's for Beauty was quite a place. And what made it so special was the beautiful people who worked there.

The address I had for the Northern Development offices turned out to be a stone-and-brick commercial building on Yuba and California streets, not far from the mall. The directory in the lobby sent me up to the second floor, where I found a pebbled-glass door with some fancy gilt lettering on it that said:

NORTHERN DEVELOPMENT CORPORATION
"GROWTH + EXPANSION = PROSPERITY"
Munroe Randall, President
M.J. Treacle, Vice President
F.L. O'Daniel, Vice President

Very impressive. And what was on the other side of the door was impressive, too—a nice front for a company wobbling on the edge of Chapter Eleven. The anteroom was about twenty feet square, paneled in blond wood and outfitted with chrome-pipe furniture covered in some kind of black-and-white cloth. Behind a desk directly opposite was a slender woman in her thirties; but she wasn't sitting down, she was standing up near one of two unmarked doors in a pose that suggested she'd been eavesdropping on what was going on behind it. Which was an argument between two men, apparently, because both voices were raised and had an angry buzz to them, like disturbed bees. What they were saying to each other wasn't quite distinguishable.

The woman turned away from the door, but not as if it mattered much to her that I'd caught her with her ears flapping. She had tawny hair cut short, brown eyes, the kind of nose that is called patrician, a nice body encased in a green shift, and a secretarial air of cool efficiency. One of those little metal-and-wood nameplates on her desk identified her as Shirley Irwin.

She said, "Yes, may I help you?"

"I'm here to see Mr. O'Daniel."

"Have you an appointment?"

"More or less. He's expecting me."

"Your name, please?"

I told her my name. She recognized it, but it didn't impress her much; I didn't impress her much either. The only thing about me that interested her seemed to be my mustache. At least, that was what her gaze kept fastening on.

"Mr. O'Daniel is in conference at the moment," she said. "Will you wait?"

"Some conference," I said, smiling.

"I beg your pardon?"

"All that shouting." I realized I was stroking the mustache and quit that; but Miss Irwin kept right on staring at it. The voices in the other room seemed to be getting louder and angrier.

"Will you wait, sir?"

"Sure. But would you mind letting Mr. O'Daniel know I'm here?"

"Mr. O'Daniel asked that he not be disturbed."

"I see. It makes me look like Groucho Marx, right?"

"What?"

"The mustache. Groucho Marx."

"I'm sure I don't know what you're talking about."

"You keep staring at it. It's not that bad, is it?"

"I couldn't care less about your facial hair," she said in a voice you could have used to chill beer.

I caught myself starting to stroke it again—and one of the men behind the door said distinctly, "I don't have to take that kind of crap from you! By God, I don't!"

I looked at the door; so did Miss Irwin. I could feel the skin across my neck pull tight.

The other man yelled, "Get away from me! Goddamn you, get away—!"

"I'll fix you once and for all, you son of a bitch!"

There was a sharp thudding sound: and there were thrashing noises, and the second man let out a half-strangled cry.

"Help! Help!"

Some of Miss Irwin's coolly efficient facade had melted and she had her hand up to her mouth. She said, "Frank!" and started for the door, but I got there ahead of her, yanked it open, and went barreling into Frank O'Daniel's private office like Fearless Fosdick to the rescue.

FIVE

They were over at a big executive's desk set in front of a sunlit window. One of them, bigger by fifty pounds, wearing Levi's and a denim shirt, had the other sprawled backward across the desk and was choking him and whacking his head against the glass top. The desk chair had been upended, a scatter of dislodged papers and paraphernalia and the remains of a glass water pitcher were on the carpet, and the telephone receiver dangled free over the desk's side. The one getting himself choked, a little guy in a white linen suit, kept trying to catch hold of the receiver, to use it as a weapon; he kept trying to kick and punch the big one too. But he couldn't get enough leverage to do any damage in return. His eyes bulged and his face had begun to mottle. He made terrified squawking sounds, like a mauled chicken.

I kept moving while I took all of this in. The heavy guy heard me coming and jerked his head around, but even when I got to him and caught hold of his shoulder, he didn't let go of the little man's neck. Instead he tried to shrug me off the way you'd rid yourself of a pesky insect; his eyes were full of blind fury. I hung onto him one-handed, got a grip on his shirt with my other hand, set myself, and used all my weight and strength to break his hold and wrench him aside. He staggered halfway across the room, ran into a chair, and fell over it. When he hit the floor it was like a small building collapsing.

The little guy squirmed around on the desk, holding his throat and squawking some more. Miss Irwin ran over to him; hauled him into a sitting position and tugged his hand away so she could check on how much damage had been done. I took her actions to mean that he was Frank O'Daniel—not that I'd had much doubt of it.

I kept my attention on the big man. He was up on all fours now, shaking his head, looking dazed; there wasn't any way to tell yet what he might do next. He was around fifty, powerfully built, going bald on top, with not much neck and not much chin. Running to fat, though. Even when he was on his feet, his paunch would hide the belt buckle on his Levi's.

I said to Miss Irwin, "Your boss okay?"

"He's bruised but he'll be all right."

"He need a doctor?"

"I don't think so."

"This man here—you know him?"

"Yes. His name is Coleclaw."

"Jack Coleclaw? From Musket Creek?"

"Yes."

"Why the attack? Any idea?"

She shook her head, looking at O'Daniel again. His squawks had tapered off into a series of heavy panting breaths: hyperventilation. Miss Irwin got him up off the desk and helped him over to the window and hoisted the sash to let in some fresh air. She held him steady, saying, "Breathe deeply and slowly. That's right. Deeply and slowly."

The big guy, Coleclaw, was upright now, but there wasn't going to be any more trouble. The fury had been jarred out of him; he wore a stunned expression, as if he couldn't believe what he'd just tried to do to O'Daniel. He looked over at the developer, looked at me, and said in a hollow voice, "Christ. I didn't mean . . . I wouldn't have . . ." Then he clamped his mouth shut, rolled his eyes, pivoted, and lumbered out of there.

I thought about trying to stop him, but I didn't feel like any more roughhousing. Besides, we all knew his name and where he lived. So I let him go. A couple of seconds later the outer door banged shut, and as soon as it did O'Daniel got his breath back and started making noise.

"He tried to strangle me! You saw it, Shirley—he tried to *murder* me! He's crazy! They're all madmen out there!"

I said, "Take it easy, Mr. O'Daniel."

He managed to get his eyes focused on me. "You saved my life," he said. "I could be dead now if you hadn't come running in."

"Maybe he wouldn't have gone that far."

"He damned near crushed my windpipe," O'Daniel said. Then he frowned and said, "Who are you, anyway? I don't know you."

I told him who I was. He said, "Oh. Sure. Well, I'm glad you showed up when you did. That Coleclaw—I tell you, he's a lunatic."

"Then maybe you'd better call the police."

"The police? No, absolutely not."

"Why not? Coleclaw attacked you, didn't he? If he *is* a lunatic he ought to be locked up."

"No police," O'Daniel said. He had his composure back now. "My God, we've had enough bad publicity as it is. We can't afford any more notoriety."

Miss Irwin said, "But what if he comes back?" She was sitting on her heels, gathering up the stuff that had been swept off the desk during the struggle.

He shook his head at her. "I'm not going to worry about that right now. Shirley . . . get me a glass of water and a shot of brandy, will you? My throat feels raw."

She straightened, put the papers and things on the desk, hung up the telephone receiver, and then went to a set of cabinet doors in one wall and opened them to reveal a wet bar. While she was getting his drinks I righted O'Daniel's desk chair and pushed it over to him. He sat down in it, wincing. He was the bantam type—five and a half feet tall, maybe a hundred and forty pounds. He had bushy brown hair going gray at the temples, bright feral eyes, and a mouth like an ax chip in a piece of light-grained wood. There was a fancy silver ring on the little finger of his left hand. He sat there plucking and fussing at his rumpled silk shirt and his white linen suit coat. He didn't look like any accountant I had ever seen before.

I said, "You mind telling me why Coleclaw attacked you?"

"Why? I told you, he's crazy."

"Well, something must have provoked him."

O'Daniel hesitated. Then he grimaced and sighed a little and said, "Oh, what the hell. It was that fucking letter."

"Letter?"

"It came this morning. I'm just not going to stand for shit like that."

"A threatening letter?"

"Yes."

"Anonymous?"

"What else."

"And you accused Coleclaw of writing it?"

"Him or one of those other buggers in Musket Creek. It was postmarked in Weaverville, the nearest town with a post office."

"Coleclaw denied it, I suppose."

"Sure he denied it. He blew up, and I blew up, and the next thing I knew the son of a bitch was strangling me."

I sat down in one of the visitors' chairs, a twin of the chrome jobs out in the anteroom. "Why did Coleclaw come here in the first place?" I asked.

"He wanted to talk about our development plans for the Musket Creek area. Try to work out a compromise of some kind, he said. He showed up out of the blue—no appointment or anything. I should've known better than to see him."

"What sort of compromise did he have in mind?"

"Something he and his crazy friends drew up. A list of restrictions as to what we could and couldn't develop, things they want to preserve in their goddamn natural state. If we agreed to it, they'd quit fighting us."

"What did you say to that?"

"I told him to go to hell," O'Daniel said. "That list of his was as long as your arm. It'd cost thousands to revamp our plans, and for what? Just to satisfy the whims of a bunch of backwoods cretins."

Miss Irwin brought him his water and his brandy. He drank the water first, gargling it a little and rubbing his throat while it went down. Then he tossed off the brandy. "Better," he said. "My head still hurts, though. You got any aspirin, Shirley?"

"I'll see."

He watched her walk out of the office. In a smarmy undertone he said to me, "Some ass, huh?"

So are you, I thought.

The telephone rang. Miss Irwin picked up out front, held a brief conversation, and then poked her head back into the office. "Your wife," she called to O'Daniel.

"Ah, Christ." He looked and sounded annoyed. "Tell her I'm busy, I'll call her back later."

"I told her that. She said it's important and it won't wait."

O'Daniel muttered something profane and plucked up the handset on his phone. "Helen? What's so damned important it can't . . . What? Yeah, I know, I know. But I can't talk about that right now. . . . Because I can't, that's why. . . ."

One of the things that had been knocked off the desk in the fight was a photograph in a silver frame. Miss Irwin had set it facing outward when she'd cleaned up the carpet, and from where I was sitting I could see that it was a color portrait of a woman that was probably Helen O'Daniel. I gave it my attention while I pretended not to listen to O'Daniel's end of the phone conversation. She was somewhere between thirty-five and forty, dark-haired, attractive in a snooty, pinch-faced way. Her mouth was smiling but her eyes weren't: that kind of woman.

"No, not tonight," O'Daniel was saying to her. "I told you before, I'm going to spend the weekend on the houseboat. . . . No, I'm not coming home, I'm leaving for the lake straight from here. . . . What? All right, all right. I'll call you."

He rang off without saying good-bye. "Shirley!" he yelled. "Where the hell's that aspirin?" Then he looked at me and said, "Women. They're a pain in the ass sometimes."

I wasn't ready or willing to discuss women with Frank O'Daniel—particularly not his wife and her possible affair with Munroe Randall. There were less direct, less inoffensive ways to find out whether or not there was any truth to Penny Belson's intimations.

I said, "Let's get back to that threatening letter you received. Do you still have it?"

"Somewhere in this mess. You want to see it?"

"If you don't mind."

He shuffled among the papers Miss Irwin had picked up, found an envelope, and handed it over. Plain white dime-store envelope, with O'Daniel's name and the company address printed in an exaggerated child's hand—somebody's method of disguising his handwriting. No return address, of course. The envelope had been slit at one end; I shook out the single sheet of paper it contained. It had been torn off a ruled yellow pad, and its message had been printed in the same scrawly hand:

> *Frank O'Daniel,*
> *If you don't leave Musket Creek alone you'll wish your mother never had you. Look what happened to your partner Randall. Don't let anything like that happen to you. Get out NOW! OR ELSE!*

When I looked up from the paper Miss Irwin was back with some aspirin and another glass of water. I waited until O'Daniel was done swallowing before I asked him, "Have there been other letters like this?"

"No. This is the first one."

"Other threats of any kind?"

"Well . . . not exactly."

"How do you mean, 'not exactly'?"

"There were a bunch of hang-up calls," he said. "Back when we first started buying up land in Musket Creek. Every time you'd pick up the phone, the bastard on the other end would hang up."

"Just here? Or at your home too?"

"Both. You remember, Shirley? A fucking nuisance."

"I remember," she said.

"It went on for a couple of weeks," O'Daniel said. "I had my home number changed finally, unlisted, but we couldn't do that here."

"No other calls since then?"

"No. They just stopped and that was it."

I tucked the anonymous letter back into its envelope, but I didn't give it back to O'Daniel. ''Were either of your partners ever threatened? Letters, calls, in person?''

''Ray Treacle was. An artist named Robideaux who lives over there threatened him to his face.''

''Yes, he told me about that. What about Munroe Randall? Was *he* ever threatened?''

''Not that he mentioned to me.''

I said bluntly, ''Do you think he was murdered, Mr. O'Daniel?''

''Munroe? Hell, I don't know what to think.''

''This letter you just got hints that maybe he was.''

O'Daniel didn't say anything for a time. You could see the wheels turning inside his head: thinking about that hundred-thousand dollar double indemnity payoff, probably. ''The police say it was an accident,'' he said at length. ''They ought to know, shouldn't they?''

''The police overlook things sometimes. Everybody does.''

''Yeah, I guess so. But that note—it could just be a crank thing. I mean, whoever wrote it might *want* me to think Munroe was murdered. You know, trying to take advantage of the accident. That could be it.''

''It could be,'' I admitted. ''But I'd like to keep the note anyway, if that's all right with you.''

''Sure, go ahead.''

I put the envelope into my coat pocket. ''Let's assume that Jack Coleclaw didn't write it,'' I said. ''Any other candidates?''

''Anybody in Musket Creek, just about.''

''The letter's fairly literate. Whoever wrote it has a pretty fair grasp of English fundamentals.''

''Well . . . Penrose, maybe.''

''Who's Penrose?''

''A writer. Writes stuff on natural history. All writers are nuts, but that one is a real fruitcake. You'll see what I mean when you talk to him.''

''That should be pretty soon,'' I said. ''I'm going out there tomorrow.''

''If I were you,'' O'Daniel said, ''I'd take along a couple of cops. They don't like strangers, particularly strangers asking questions that have anything to do with Northern Development.''

''It can't be that bad, Mr. O'Daniel.''

"No?" He put a hand up to his throat. "Well, it's *your* neck this time, not mine."

Kerry was out by the pool, soaking up the last of the dying sun, when I got back to the Sportsman's Rest. She was in better spirits too, which was a relief. She wanted to know all about my day, and she kept asking questions and chattering at me the whole time we were getting ready to go out for dinner.

But by the time we picked out a restaurant, her mood had shifted. Periods of silence again, interspersed with grouchy comments on the food, the decor, my table manners, and the feeble quality of my jokes. She didn't say much on the ride back to the motel, and nothing at all for the first half hour we were in the room.

I figured it was going to be a long evening, so I got out the three typed, single-spaced sheets Shirley Irwin had given me before I'd left the Northern Development offices, and read up on the citizens of Musket Creek. But pretty soon Kerry's mood shifted again, and when she got into bed she wanted to make love. So we did, and she was half-wild about it, exhausting both of us, and afterward she clung to me and said the things lovers say to each other and apologized for being so moody and said she'd be much better company for the rest of the trip.

Only then I made the mistake of asking her what it was that was troubling her, and she shut up again and turned away from me and pretended to go to sleep.

I lay there staring up at the dark ceiling, feeling sorry for myself and thinking that Eberhardt was right: I don't understand women worth a damn.

SIX

The road that led off State Highway 299 to Musket Creek was not only unpaved; it was rutted, narrow, full of dips and hairpin turns, and so dusty in places you felt as though you were driving through a kind of talcum-powder mist. The terrain was mountainous, heavily forested, with small open meadows here and there that were carpeted with wild clover and purple-blue lupine—scenic, yet without any spectacular vistas. Far off to the east you could see the immense snow-capped peak of Mt. Shasta jutting more than 14,000 feet into the cloud-flecked sky. But that was a commonplace sight in this country; on a clear day, that granddaddy of mountains was visible from just about anywhere within a fifty-mile radius.

Beside me, Kerry kept putting her head out of the open passenger window and sniffing the air like a cat. She was in a pretty good mood today, and she seemed to be enjoying herself so far—living up to last night's promise. She had insisted on coming along; she hadn't felt like sitting around the motel alone, she'd said, and she was curious about Ragged-Ass Gulch. So I'd given in and let her come, to keep the peace between us, but I wasn't sure it was such a hot idea. I kept thinking about Jack Coleclaw's attack on O'Daniel yesterday, all the things I'd been told about the "loonies" of Musket Creek. There probably wasn't anything to worry about; hell, you could classify both O'Daniel and Treacle as loonies, if you felt like it. But it still made me a little trepidatious.

The road seemed to go on endlessly. The car's odometer showed 7.2 miles when the dusty strip slanted between a couple of high, wooded cliffs and the mountains folded back finally to reveal a little valley down below. And there it was—Musket Creek in all its glory.

The valley floor had a rippled look, full of hillocks, like a bright green carpet that had been bunched in at both ends to make a series of wrinkles. The town—such as it was—lay sprawled toward the far end, where the narrow line of the creek meandered through high grass, wildflowers, and stands of fir trees. Some of the buildings had been built on the hummocks; what looked to be the main street of the old mining ghost town was on flat ground paralleling the creek. Most of the buildings were tumbledown—and off to the left I could see the blackened skeletons of the four that had burned ten days ago—but at a distance the sunlight and the majestic surroundings softened the look of them, gave them a kind of nostalgic quaintness.

Kerry said, "Why, it's beautiful," in a surprised voice. "No wonder the people who live here don't want the place developed."

"Yeah," I said.

We went on a ways. Then she said, "Why would anybody in his right mind call such an idyllic spot Ragged-Ass Gulch?"

"Somebody's idea of a joke, maybe. Miners had oddball senses of humor."

"That's for sure."

When we reached the meadow the road deteriorated into little more than a pair of ruts with a grassy hump in the middle. It angled off to the right and eventually forked; one branch became the single main street of the old camp, passing between facing rows of its abandoned buildings, and the other hooked over and disappeared onto the rising ground to the west. According to the information supplied by Shirley Irwin, more people lived back there in the woods.

The first buildings we came to were before the fork, on a long stretch of level ground—a combination single-pump gas station, garage and body shop, and general store. The garage and store were weathered and unpainted, but in a decent state of repair. A couple of hand-lettered signs hung over the screen-doored entrance to the latter; the big one said MUSKET CREEK MERCANTILE and the little one said BAIT • TACKLE • AMMUNITION • GUIDE SERVICE. The garage wall was plastered with old metal Coca-Cola and beer signs. Around back, to one side, was a frame cottage with a big native-stone chimney at one end. The folks who lived in the cottage and ran the businesses were the Coleclaws: Jack, his wife, and their son Gary.

I decided I might as well get my talk with Jack Coleclaw out of the way first, so I pulled in off the road and stopped next to the gas pump. A fat brown-and-white dog came around from behind the store, took one look at the car, and began barking its head off. No one else appeared.

"I'd better do this alone," I said to Kerry. "You wait in the car."

"All right."

I got out, keeping my eye on the dog. It continued to bark, but it didn't make any sudden moves in my direction. I took the fact that its tail was wagging to be a positive sign and started toward the entrance to the store.

Just before I got there, a pudgy young guy in grease-stained overalls appeared in the doorway of the garage. "Be quiet, Sam," he said to the dog. He didn't say anything to me, or move out of the doorway. And the dog went right on yapping.

I walked over to where the young guy stood. He was in his middle twenties and he had curly brown hair and pink beardless cheeks and big doe eyes that had a remote look in them. The eyes watched me without curiosity as I came up to him.

"Hi," I said. "You're Gary Coleclaw, right?"

"Yeah," he said.

"I'd like to talk to your father, if he's around."

"He's not. He went to Weaverville this morning."

"When will he be back?"

He shrugged. "This afternoon sometime."

"How about your mother? Is she here?"

"No. She went to Weaverville too."

"Well, maybe you can help me. I'm a detective, from San Francisco, and I—"

"Detective?" he said.

"Yes. I'm investigating the death of Munroe Randall in Redding—"

"The Northern guy," he said. His face closed up; you could see it happening, like watching a poppy fold its petals at sundown. "The fire. I don't know nothing about that. Except he got what was coming to him."

"Is that what your father says too?"

"That's what everybody says. Listen, mister, you working for them? Them Northern guys?"

"No."

"Yeah, you are. Them damn Northern guys."

"No, I'm working for the insurance—"

But he had pivoted away from me, was hurrying back inside the garage. I called after him, "Hey, wait," but he didn't stop or turn.

An old black Chrysler sat on the floor inside, its front end jacked up; there was one of those little wheeled mechanic's carts alongside, and he dropped down onto it on his back and scooted himself under the Chrysler until only his legs were showing. A moment later I heard the sharp, angry sound of some kind of tool whacking against the undercarriage.

The damned dog was still barking. I sidestepped it and went back to the car. When I slid in under the wheel Kerry asked, "Well?"

"He wouldn't talk to me. And his folks aren't here."

"What now?"

"The fire," I said.

I drove out along the road again. Just beyond the right fork, two more occupied cottages sat on adjacent hummocks, like odd-shaped nipples on a pair of big breasts. The nearest one had a deserted look, but in the yard of the second, a heavy-set woman of about seventy, wearing man's clothing and a straw hat, was wielding a hoe among tall rows of tomato vines. She stopped when she heard the car and stood staring out at the road as we passed by, as if she resented the appearance of strangers in Musket Creek.

Kerry said, "None of the natives is very friendly, the way it looks."

"So I've been warned."

I kept on going along the right fork, through what was left of the mining camp. It amounted to about two blocks' worth of buildings on both sides of the road, although here and there in the surrounding meadows you could see foundations and other remains of what had once been additional structures. Most of the buildings still standing were backed up against the creek. There were about fifteen altogether, all made of whipsawn boards on stone foundations, some reinforced with tin siding and roofs, a third with badly decayed frames and collapsing eaves. The largest—two-storied, girdled by a sagging and partly missing veranda at the second level—looked to have been either a hotel or a saloon with upstairs accommodations; it bore no signs other than one somebody had painted on its sheet metal roof, advertising Bull Durham tobacco. Several of the others did have signs, or what was left of them: UNION DRUG STORE, MEAT MARKET, MINER'S HALL; M. SANDERS & SON, BLACKSMITHS; MUSKET CREEK GENERAL MERCHANDISE & HARDWARE, S. WILBUR, PROP.

As far as I could tell as we passed, all their doors and windows were either boarded up or sealed with tacked-on sheets of tin.

Kerry seemed impressed. "This is some place," she said. "I've never been in a ghost town before."

"Spooky, huh?"

"No. I'm fascinated. How long have these buildings been here?"

"Well over a century, some of them."

"And people have been living here all that time and nobody ever tried to restore them?"

"Not in a good long while."

"Well, why not? I mean, you'd think *somebody* would want to preserve a historic place like this."

"Somebody does," I said. "The Northern Development Corporation."

"I don't mean that kind of preservation. You know what I mean."

"Uh-huh. It's a good question, but I don't know the answer."

She frowned a little, thoughtfully. "What kind of people live here, anyway?"

"That's another good question. I guess we'll find out pretty soon."

The four fire-destroyed buildings had been set apart from the others, on the south side of the road. That, along with the facts that there had been no wind on the night of the blaze, that the meadow grass was still spring-green, and that Jack Coleclaw and the other residents had spotted the fire right away and rushed to do battle with it, had saved the whole of the abandoned camp from going up. As it was, there was nothing left of the four structures except stone foundations and timber fragments like blackened and splintered bones, with a wide swatch of scorched earth and a hastily dug firebreak ringing them.

I stopped the car at the edge of the firebreak. Kerry said, "I suppose you're going to go poke around over there."

"Yup. Come along if you want to."

"In all that soot? No thanks. I think I'll go back and look at the ghosts."

We got out into the hot sunshine. It was quiet there, peaceful except for the distant yammering of a jay, and the air was heavy with the scent of wildflowers and evergreens. Kerry wandered off along the road; I took out the old, soot-stained trenchcoat I'd worn in Redding, put it on and belted it, and then went across the firebreak to the burned-out buildings.

The county sheriff's investigators had been over the area without finding anything; I didn't expect to have better luck, any more than I had at the remains of Munroe Randall's house. But then, I'd had some training in arson investigation myself, back when I was on the San Francisco cops, and I read the updated handbooks and manuals put out by police associations and insurance companies. I had also had a handful of jobs over the years involving arson. You have to keep checking and double-checking: that's what detective work is all about.

The first thing you do on an inspection of a fire scene is to determine the point of origin. Once you've got that, you look for something to indicate how the fire started, whether it was accidental or a case of arson. If it was arson, what you're after is the corpus delicti—evidence of the method or device used by the arsonist.

One of the ways to locate point of origin is to check the "alligatoring," or charring, of the surface of the burned wood. This can tell you in which direction the fire spread, where it was the hottest, and if you're fortunate you can trace it straight to the origin. I was fortunate, as it turned out. And not just once—twice. I not only found the point of origin, I found the corpus delicti as well.

It was arson, and no mistake. The fire had been set at the rear of the building farthest to the north, whatever that one might once have been; and what had been used to ignite it was a candle. I found the residue of it, a wax deposit inside a small cup-shaped piece of stone that was hidden under a pile of rubble. It took me ten minutes of sifting around and getting my hands and the trenchcoat completely blackened to dredge up the stone. Which was no doubt why the sheriff's men hadn't been as thorough as they should have been; not everybody is willing to turn himself into the likeness of a chimney sweep, particularly on a minor fire out in the middle of nowhere.

As near as I could determine, the candle had been made of purple-colored tallow. Which told me nothing much; purple candles were not uncommon. It had probably been stuck inside the cup-shaped stone to keep it from toppling over and starting the fire before it was intended to.

I was peering at the stone, and it wasn't telling me much either, when I heard and then saw the jeep come up. It rattled to a stop behind my car, and a guy about six-four unfolded from behind the wheel and plunked himself down on the road. He stared over at me for a couple of seconds, shading his eyes against the sun. Then he yelled, "Hey! You there! What do you think you're doing?"

I saw no point in yelling back at him. Instead I put the stone into my trenchcoat pocket, swatted some of the soot off my hands, then made my way through the rubble and across to where the guy stood alongside his jeep. He was in his forties, beanpole thin, with a shock of fiery red hair and a belligerent expression to match it. Behind him in the jeep I could see a folded easel, a couple of blank three-foot-square canvases, and a box that probably contained brushes and oil paints.

When I stopped in front of him he scowled down at me and said, "What's the idea of messing around over there? You a scavenger or something?"

"No," I said, "I'm a detective."

"A what?"

"A detective." I told him who I was and where I was from and that I had been hired to investigate the death of Munroe Randall.

He didn't like hearing it. His expression got even more belligerent; his eyes were flat and shiny-black, like circlets of onyx. "Who hired you? Northern Development?"

"No. The insurance company that carries the policy on Randall's life."

"So what the hell are you doing here? Randall died in a fire in Redding."

"You had a fire here too," I said.

"Coincidence."

"Maybe not, Mr. Robideaux."

"How do you know my name?"

"I know the names of everybody who lives here. The Northern people supplied them."

"I'll bet they did."

"The list includes an artist named Paul Robideaux." I nodded toward the paraphernalia in the jeep. "I get paid to observe things and make educated guesses."

Robideaux grunted and screwed up his mouth as if he wanted to spit. He didn't say anything.

I said, "I'd like to ask you a few questions about the fire."

"Which fire?"

"This one. Unless you know something about the one in Redding too."

"I don't know anything about either one. I wasn't in Redding when Randall's place burned. And I wasn't here when those old shacks went up."

"No? That isn't what you told the county sheriff's men. According to their report, you were one of the residents who helped dig the firebreak."

"Is that so?" Robideaux said. "Well, I had to talk to the law. I don't have to talk to you."

"That's right, you don't. But suppose I told you I can prove this fire was deliberately set. Would you want to talk to me then?"

His eyes got narrow. "How could you prove that? You find something in the debris?"

"Maybe."

"What is it?"

"I have to tell that to the law," I said. "I don't have to tell it to you."

He took a jerky half-step toward me, the menacing kind. I stayed where I was, setting myself; he was not big enough for me to be intimidated. But if he'd had any ideas about mixing it up, he thought better of them. He turned abruptly and stalked around to the driver's side of the jeep.

Only he didn't get in right away. Instead he pointed a finger in my direction and said, "You think Randall was murdered, is that it? Well, why don't you go sniff around those partners of his? One of them killed him if anybody did."

"Why do you say that?"

"Because nobody here did it, that's why. There's nothing for you in Musket Creek."

"Nothing but trouble, you mean?"

"You said it, I didn't."

He got into the jeep. Fifteen seconds later he was barreling off down the road, trailing dust, headed toward the pines to the west.

I stood staring after him. And wondering, not for the first time in the past two days, if there wasn't a lot more going on in this business than I'd first thought.

SEVEN

Kerry still hadn't come back. Between my search of the fire wreckage and my conversation with Robideaux, over an hour had passed since she'd wandered off. I looked over at the ghosts, but there was no sign of her. Now what's she up to? I wondered. I shed my trenchcoat, locked it and the wax-laden stone cup into the trunk, used a rag to wipe off my hands, and set out looking for her.

She wasn't anywhere on the south side of the street. I crossed over, went down a weed-choked alleyway between two of the derelicts. The grass was high back there, a field of it extending thirty yards or so to the creek. A railed footbridge spanned the shallow but swift-moving stream; on the other side, a pair of half-obliterated ruts led up one of the hillocks to a collapsed building at its crest—what had once been a church or a schoolhouse, judging from the remains of a belltower. Pieces of machinery, the segments of a sluicebox, and other broken and rusted mining equipment littered the grass on both sides of the creek. Some of it was so badly weathered and busted up that you couldn't tell what it had been used for.

An irregular path led through the grass from the footbridge and intersected another path that paralleled the rear of the buildings. I got onto the parallel one and went along calling Kerry's name. She finally answered me from inside one of the ghosts—the two-storied hotel or saloon. The back entrance wasn't boarded up the way the front was and the door hung open on one hinge; I went inside.

She was standing in the middle of a big, gloomy, high-ceilinged room. Enough sunlight penetrated, through chinks where the wall boards had warped away from the studs, to let me see what the room had to offer. Not much. A balcony ran around three sides at the second-floor level, with three doorways sans doors opening off it on the left side and three more on the right; the balcony sagged badly in places and looked as though it might topple at any time. So did the crooked staircase leaning in one corner down at this level. The floor looked like what was left of a junk shop that had gone out of business. Some old broken chairs and tables; the rusty skeleton of a sheet-iron stove and its piping; the door to a steel safe, circa 1880, with faded gold lettering on it that said *Diebold, Norris & Co., Chicago*; a native-stone fireplace with most of the stones lying mounded on the hearth; a crudely made hotel reception desk, part of which was hidden by a pigeonhole shelf that had collapsed on top of it; and random piles of dirt and other detritus.

"What'd you do?" I asked Kerry. "Bust in here?"

"No. The back door was ajar. Isn't this place wonderful?"

"If you like dust, decay, and rats."

"Rats? There aren't any rats in here."

"Want to bet?"

Rats didn't scare her much, though. She shrugged and said, "Somebody lives in this building."

"What?"

"Well, maybe not lives here, but spends a lot of time here. That's how come the back door isn't boarded up."

"How did you find this out?"

"The same way you find things out," she said. "By snooping around. Come on, I'll show you."

She led me over behind the hotel desk, to where a closed door was half-concealed by the fallen pigeonhole shelf. "The door's got an almost-new latch on it," she said, pointing. "See? That made me curious, so I opened it to see what was inside."

She opened it again as she spoke and let *me* see what was inside. It was a room maybe twelve-by-twelve that had probably been built for the hotel clerk's use. There was a boarded-up window in the far wall; two of the other three walls were bare; the third one, to the left, had a long six-foot-high tier of standing shelves, like an unfinished bookcase, leaning against it. The shelves were crammed with all sorts of odds and ends, the bulk of which seemed to be Indian arrowheads, chunks of iron pyrite or fool's gold, rocks with designs, rocks that gleamed with mica or maybe genuine gold particles, and curious-shaped bits of wood. An army cot with a straw-tick mattress, a Coleman lantern, and an upended wooden box supporting several tattered issues of *National Geographic* completed the furnishings.

"Pack rats," I said. "That's who lives here."

Kerry frowned at me.

"Either that, or a small-scale junk dealer."

She said, "Phooey. Where's your sense of mystery and adventure? Why couldn't it be an old prospector with a gold mine somewhere up in the hills?"

"There aren't any gold mines up in the hills—not any more. Besides, if anybody had one, what would he want to come all the way down here for?"

"To forage for food, maybe."

"Hah," I said. "Well, whoever bunks in this place might just get upset if he showed up and found us in his bedroom. Technically we're trespassing. We'd better go; I've got work to do."

This time she made a face at me. "Sometimes," she said, "you're about as much fun as a pimple on the fanny."

"Kerry, I'm on a job. The fun can come later."

"Oh, you think so? Maybe not."

"Is that a threat to withhold your sexual favors?"

"Sexual favors," she said. "My, how you talk."

"You didn't answer my question."

"It was a dumb question. I don't answer dumb questions."

She started back across the hotel lobby, leaving me to shut the door to the pack rat's nest. Outside, we walked in silence to where the car was parked. But once we got inside she pointed over at the burned-out buildings and asked, "Did you find anything?" and she sounded cheerful again.

I sighed a little. Being with Kerry sometimes made me feel as if my head were as full of dusty junk as that room inside the hotel. And that no matter how long I tried, I would never quite get it all sorted out and put where it belonged.

I told her about the melted candle, explaining how I'd found it. She said she thought I was very clever; I decided not to tell her that my methods had been devised by somebody else. I also mentioned my conversation with Robideaux. By the time I was finished with that I had the car nosing up the little hill toward the second cottage near the fork, the one where the elderly woman was still hoeing among her tomato vines.

The woman's name, according to the intelligence sheets I'd been given, was Ella Bloom. She and her husband had moved here in the late 1950s, after he sold his plumbing supply company in Eureka in order to pursue a lifelong ambition to pan for gold. He'd never found much of it, evidently, but Mrs. Bloom must have liked it here anyway; she'd stayed on following his death eight years ago.

She quit hoeing and glared out at us as she had earlier. She was tall and angular, and she had a nose like the blade of her hoe and long straggly black hair. Put a tall-crowned hat on her head and a broomstick instead of the hoe in her hand, I thought, and she could have passed for the Wicked Witch of the West.

I got out of the car, went up to the gate in the picket fence that enclosed the yard. I put on a smile and called to her, "Mrs. Bloom?"

"Who are you?" she said suspiciously.

I gave her my name. "I'm an investigator working for Great Western Insurance on the death of Munroe Randall—"

That was as far as I got. The way she reacted, you'd have thought I had told her I intended to rape her and pillage her house. She hoisted up the hoe, waved it over her head, and whacked it down into the ground like an executioner's sword; then she hoisted it again and jabbed it in my direction.

"Get away from here!" she said in a thin, screechy voice. "Go on, get away!"

"Look, Mrs. Bloom, I only want to ask you a couple of questions—"

"I got nothing to say to you or anybody else about *them.* You come into my yard, mister, you'll regret it. I got a shotgun in the house and I keep it loaded."

"There's no need for—"

"You want to see it? By God, I'll show it to you if that's what it takes!"

She threw down the hoe and went flying across the yard, up onto a porch decorated with painted milk cans, and inside the house. I hesitated for about two seconds and then moved back to the car. There wasn't much sense in waiting there for her to come out with her shotgun; she wasn't going to talk, and for all I knew she was loopy enough to start blasting away at me.

"Christ," I said when I slid into the car. "That woman's not playing with a full deck."

Kerry had heard it all but she wasn't even ruffled. "I don't think so. Maybe she's got a right to act that way."

"What?"

"If somebody was trying to turn my home into a cheap imitation of Disneyland I'd be pretty mad about it too."

"Yeah," I said, "but you wouldn't start threatening people for no damn reason."

"I might, if I were her age."

"Bah," I said. But because Mrs. Bloom had reappeared with a bulky twelve-gauge cradled in both hands, I started the car and swung it into a fast U-turn. Kerry might not have been worried, but she'd never been shot at and I had. People with guns make me nervous, no matter who they are.

EIGHT

The cottage on the adjacent hillock was owned by a couple named Brewster, but with Mrs. Bloom and her shotgun nearby, this was not the time to talk to them. The atmosphere in Musket Creek was every bit as hostile as Frank O'Daniel had suggested it would be; bringing Kerry along had definitely not been a good idea. I considered calling it quits for now and heading back to Redding. But if I did, Kerry would never let me hear the end of it—and I couldn't believe that everybody up here was screwy enough to threaten us. I decided to try interviewing one more resident. If that went as badly as my other attempts had, then the hell with it and I would come back tomorrow alone.

At the fork I took the left branch that led away from town and up into the wooded slopes to the west. The first house we came to belonged to Paul Robideaux; the second, almost a mile farther along, was a free-form cabin that resembled a somewhat lopsided A-frame, built on sloping ground and bordered on three sides by tall redwoods and Douglas fir. It had been pieced together with salvaged lumber, rough-hewn beams, native stone, redwood thatch, and inexpensive plate glass. A woodbutcher's house, woodbutchers being people who went off to homestead in the wilds because they didn't like cities, mass-produced housing, or most people.

When I slowed and eased the car off the road next to a parked Land Rover, Kerry asked, "Who lives here?"

"Hugh Penrose. He's a writer."

"What does he write?"

"Articles and books on natural history. He used to be a professor at Chico State. Apparently he's an eccentric."

"Mmm. How about letting me come with you this time? You don't seem to be doing too well one-on-one."

"I don't think that's a good idea—"

"Phooey," she said, and got out and went up toward the cabin.

Well, damn! But there was nothing I could do except to follow her, telling myself this was the *last* time I brought her along on an investigation.

We went up a set of curving limb-and-plank stairs to a platform deck. From inside I could hear the sound of a typewriter rattling away. I knocked on the door. The typewriter kept on going for half a minute; then it stopped, and there were footsteps, and pretty soon the door opened.

The guy who looked out at us was one of the ugliest men I had ever seen. He was about five and a half feet tall, fat, with a bulbous nose and misshapen ears and cheeks pitted with acne scars, and his bullet-shaped head was as bald as an egg. His eyes were small and mean, but there was more pain in them than anything else. This was a man who had lived more than fifty years, I thought, and who had suffered through every one of them.

He looked at Kerry, looked away from her as if embarrassed, and fixed his gaze on me. "Yes? What is it?"

"Mr. Penrose?"

"Yes?"

Before I could open my mouth again, Kerry said cheerfully, "We're the Wades, Bill and Kerry. From San Francisco. We're thinking of moving up here—you know, homesteading. I hope you don't mind us calling on you like this."

"How did you know my name?" Penrose asked. He was still looking at me.

"The fellow at the mercantile gave it to us," Kerry said. "He told us you were a homesteader and we thought we'd come by and look at your place and see how you liked living here."

I could have kicked her. It was one of those flimsy, spontaneous stories that sound as phony as they are. But she got away with it, by God, at least for the moment. All Penrose said was, "Which fellow at the mercantile?" and he said it without suspicion.

"Mr. Coleclaw."

"Which Mr. Coleclaw?"

"I didn't know there was more than one. He was in his twenties and the only one around." Kerry glanced at me. "Did he give you his first name, dear?"

"Gary," I said. "Dear."

"Poor young fool," Penrose said. "Poor lost lad."

"Pardon?"

"He has rocks in his head," Penrose said, and burst out laughing. The laugh went on for maybe three seconds, like the barking of a sea lion, exposing yellowed and badly fitting dentures; then it cut off as if somebody had smacked a hand over his mouth. He looked embarrassed again.

Definitely an oddball, I thought. Musket Creek seemed to be full of them, all right. But Penrose, at least, had my sympathy; the strain of coping with physical deformities like his was enough to throw anybody a little out of whack.

"That was a dreadful pun," he said. "Gary can't help it if he's retarded; I don't know what makes me so cruel sometimes. I apologize. No one should make fun of others, should they." It wasn't a question, so he didn't wait for a response. He went on, "What else did the boy tell you? Did he say anything about the Northern Development Corporation?"

Kerry simulated a blank look that would have got her thrown out of any acting school in the country. But again, Penrose didn't notice; he still wasn't looking at her, except for brief sidelong eye-flicks whenever she spoke. "No," she said, "he didn't. Is that something we should know about?"

"Yes. Oh yes. If they have their way you won't want to move

here.'' He paused. ''But I'm forgetting my manners. I haven't many visitors, you see. Would you like to come in?''

Kerry said, ''Yes, thanks. That would be nice.''

So Penrose stepped aside and we went in. The interior of the cabin—just one big room—was furnished sparsely with mismatched secondhand items and strewn with books. Against the back wall was a long table with a typewriter, a bunch of papers, and an unlit candle on it. The candle caught and held my attention. It was fat, it was stuck inside a wooden bowl, and it was purple—the same color purple as the one I'd found at the burned-out ghosts.

I went over to the table for a closer look. When Kerry finished declining Penrose's offer of a cup of coffee I said to him, ''That's a nice candle you've got there.''

''Candle?'' he said blankly.

''I wouldn't mind having one like it.'' I gave Kerry a pointed look. ''We collect candles, don't we, dear.''

''Yes, that's right. We do.''

''Did you get it locally?'' I asked Penrose.

''From a widow lady who lives here, yes.''

''May I ask her name?''

''Ella Bloom. She makes them; it's her hobby.''

''Just purple ones? Or other colors too?''

''Just purple. Her favorite color.''

''Does she sell them to anyone besides you?''

''Oh, I didn't buy it from her. She gave it to me. She doesn't make them to sell.''

''Does she give them away to everyone around here?''

''Yes. Everyone. Maybe she'll give one to you, if you ask her. Her house is right near the mercantile.''

So much for the purple-candle angle.

I steered Penrose back to the topic of Northern Development, and this time he managed to stay on it without getting sidetracked. He launched into a two-minute diatribe against the developers and what he called ''the warped values of modern society.'' He didn't seem quite as militant as Robideaux and Mrs. Bloom, but then he didn't know I was a detective.

I said, ''Isn't there anything that can be done to stop them, Mr. Penrose?''

"Well, we've hired attorneys, you know, and they've filed suit to block the sale of the land. There's nothing else to be done until the suit comes to trial."

"Have you tried appealing to the Northern people? To get them to modify their plans?"

"Oh yes. They won't listen to us. Awful people. The head of the company was an insensitive swine."

"Was?"

"He died a few days ago," Penrose said, with a hint of relish in his voice. "A tragic accident."

"What sort of accident?"

"He went to blazes." Penrose did his barking sea-lion number again. This time he didn't look quite so embarrassed when the noise stopped. "One shouldn't speak lightly of the dead, should one," he said.

"You mean he died in a fire?"

"Yes. In Redding."

"That's a coincidence," I said.

"Coincidence?"

"You had a fire here recently. We noticed the burned-out buildings on the way through."

"Oh, that. It was only four of the ghosts."

"Another accident?"

He didn't answer the question. Instead he said, "I told the others they should have let the fire spread, let it purge the other ghosts as well, but they wouldn't listen. A pity."

Kerry said, "You wanted all the buildings to burn up?"

"All the ghosts, yes."

"But why?"

"They're long dead; cremation is fitting and overdue," he said. "Ashes to ashes, dust to dust."

I said, "Shouldn't the buildings be preserved for historical reasons? After all, this was once a Gold Rush camp—"

"Definitely not. The past is dead; *requiescat in pace*. Resurrection breeds tourists." He smiled, rubbed his bulbous nose, and repeated the phrase as if he liked the sound of it: "Resurrection breeds tourists."

"Does everybody in Musket Creek feel the same way?"

"Oh, yes. Leave us alone, they say. Let us live and let us die, all in good time."

"So that's why nobody here ever tried to restore any of the buildings," Kerry said.

"Just so," Penrose agreed. "Natural history is relevant; the history of man is often irrelevant. You see?"

I asked, "How do you suppose the fire got started? The one here, I mean."

"Does it matter, Mr. Wade?"

"I'm just curious."

"Curiosity kills cats and lays ghosts," he said, and cut loose with his laugh again. Listening to it, and to his slightly whacky comments, was making me a little uncomfortable. I get just as nervous around unarmed oddballs as I do around those with weapons.

"Is it possible somebody set the fire deliberately?" I asked him. "Somebody who feels as you do about cremating the ghosts?"

It was the wrong thing to say. Penrose's mean little eyes narrowed, and when he spoke again his voice had lost its friendliness. "I think you'd better leave now. I have work to do."

Kerry said, "Couldn't we talk a while longer, Mr. Penrose? I really would like to know more about—"

"No," he said. "No. Come back and visit me again if you decide to move here. But I don't think you should; it's probably too late. Good-bye."

There was nothing for us to do but leave. We went out onto the platform deck, and Kerry thanked him for talking to us, and he said gruffly, "Not at all," and banged the door shut behind us.

On the way down the stairs she said, "Why do you always have to be so damned blunt?"

"He was getting on my nerves."

"We could have found out more if you'd been a little more tactful."

"We? 'Bill and Kerry Wade, from San Francisco.' Christ!"

"It got him to talk to us, didn't it?"

"All right, so it got him to talk to us."

"Which is more than you accomplished with your direct approach to Mrs. Bloom," she said. "You probably blurted out that you're a detective to Gary Coleclaw and that artist, Robideaux, too. No wonder they wouldn't tell you anything."

"Listen, don't tell me how to do my job."

"I'm not. I'm only suggesting—"

"Don't suggest. I didn't bring you along to do any suggesting."

"No, I know why you brought me along. Women are only good for one thing, right?"

"Oh for God's sake, I didn't mean—"

"You can be a macho jerk sometimes, you know that? You think you know everything."

She got into the car and sat there with her arms folded, staring straight ahead. I wanted to say something else to her, but I didn't seem to have any words. The thing was, she was right. I had handled things badly with Penrose, and with Gary Coleclaw and Robideaux and Mrs. Bloom. And with Kerry, too. It was just one of those days when you can't seem to get the proper handle on how to deal with anybody. But it galled me to have to admit it, and I couldn't bring myself to do it. Which was silly and petulant, but it was also a pride thing, however much of a macho jerk it made me. Kerry wasn't the detective here, damn it; *I* was.

A half-mile farther along there was another homesteader's cabin, this one owned by a family named Butterfield, but I was in no frame of mind for another Musket Creek interview. I drove back into the valley. When we came to the Coleclaw place I looked it over for some indication that Jack Coleclaw and his wife had returned from Weaverville. There wasn't any—no automobiles, no people, not even any sign of the fat yapping brown-and-white dog. So there was no point in stopping there either.

I kept on driving up the road and out of Ragged-Ass Gulch.

NINE

There was a message waiting for me at the Sportsman's Rest. And it surprised me a little when I saw who it was from: Mrs. Helen O'Daniel. She had called about ten o'clock, left a telephone number and an address, and asked that I either get in touch with her by phone or drop by any time this afternoon. She hadn't said what it was she wanted. Or, for that matter, how she'd known where I was staying, although she'd probably got that information from her husband or from Shirley Irwin.

I ruminated for about ten seconds and decided to go see her in person. I wanted a look at the lady, for one thing; and I wanted to find out if there was anything to Penny Belson's intimations of an affair between her and Munroe Randall. You can't bring up delicate matters like that on the telephone, or even do any subtle probing. Telephones are blunt instruments in more ways than one, especially among strangers.

The address she'd given me was a number on Sky Vista Road; that was a ritzy section up in the hills west of town, the motel clerk told me. I got directions from her and then returned to the room to tell Kerry where I was going. She said, "I hope you don't make an ass of yourself with her too." I sighed and went out and got into the car and drove away feeling grumpy.

It took me half an hour to find Sky Vista Road and the O'Daniel house. It was one of these split-level jobs built into the side of a hill, made out of redwood-and-brick with waves of ivy clinging to it. There was a covered platform deck that served as a garage, and parked on it was a lemon-colored Porsche with a personalized license plate that said FAST UN. You couldn't see the back end of the house from the road, because of the way it was built and because of oak and pepper trees that crowded in close on both sides; but you knew there would be wide balconies on at least two levels, with a sweeping view of the town and the mountains and Mt. Shasta in the distance.

I found a dirt turnaround to park in nearby, walked back and down some stairs to the front porch. A little card above the bell read: NO SOLICITORS. I pushed the bell anyway and stood there waiting.

The door opened before long and I was looking at the woman in the photograph on Frank O'Daniel's desk. The dark hair was piled up on her head and fastened with a barrette; she was wearing a tank top and a pair of white shorts that revealed a lot of skin the color of burnt butter. She had very good legs.

She let me look her over for about five seconds, while she did the same to me. I was more impressed by what I saw than she was, but not by much. Her expression was even more snooty than it had seemed in the photograph.

She said finally, "Yes? May I help you?"

"If you're Helen O'Daniel, maybe you can," I said, and I told her who I was.

The name worked a kind of metamorphosis on her. The snootiness vanished, her mouth got smiley, she put a hand up to touch her hair; she went a little soft-looking, too, at least around the edges. She wanted to do all of that slowly and subtly, so it didn't look like she was putting it on just for me. But she wasn't good at that sort of thing. It all seemed to come at once, like a quick-change artist shedding one costume for another: within the space of two heartbeats I was looking at a completely different version of Helen O'Daniel. I doubted if I was going to like the second one any better than the first.

"Forgive me," she said, "I didn't mean to sound rude. It's just that there have been so many interruptions today . . . and I wasn't sure if you'd call first . . ."

"I probably should have," I said, "but your message said to drop by."

"No, it's perfectly all right. I'm glad you did. Come in—we'll talk out on the deck."

She led me through a maze of white, hairy-looking furniture, suspended mobiles made out of silver doodads and colored glass, big tropical plants with thick trembly leaves that had the malevolent look of carnivores. Most of that stuff was in a massive living room or family room or whatever they call them. Part of its outer wall was made of sliding glass, open now; the other part was a brick fireplace with some weird abstract paintings mounted above the mantel. The deck beyond was about what I'd expected: a wide balcony complete with a tinted-glass sunroof and a view that had probably added another twenty thousand to the price of the house.

Mrs. O'Daniel stopped in the middle of the room and faced me again. "I was just about to have a gin and tonic," she said. "Will you join me?"

"Thanks, no."

"Something else, then? I have just about everything . . ."

"Nothing right now."

"Well. Excuse me just a second?"

"Sure."

She went out of the room through a doorway beyond the fireplace, rolling her hips a little the way she had on the way in. It wasn't an exaggerated roll, but I thought that it was deliberate. Whatever her reasons, Helen O'Daniel was about as subtle as an elephant's hind end.

I decided I didn't want to keep on standing there like another piece of furniture. Besides which, the nearest tropical plant seemed to be looking at me in a hungry sort of way. So I went and examined one of the hairy items. It was large, it was oddly shaped, it had tufts of white furry stuff sticking out of it. It looked like nothing so much as a giant rabbit that had been decapitated, stuffed, and turned into a chair.

Helen O'Daniel was still out in the kitchen; I could hear her rattling ice. I wandered over to the fireplace for a closer look at the weird paintings. One of them was tolerable: it had a sort of design and at least its riot of colors—reds and blues and blacks—didn't clash. The other one looked like somebody had vomited up a purplish succotash and stirred it around on canvas with a stick. Things like this made me glad I was a lowbrow and didn't know the first thing about art. A name was scrawled in one corner, and idle curiosity about who had perpetrated such a piece of crap made me lean down and peer at it. Only then my curiosity quit being idle and I wasn't thinking about art any more.

The name of the artist was Paul Robideaux.

Mrs. O'Daniel came back just then, carrying a tall glass. She saw me standing in front of the painting, blinked, and came to a standstill. Her face didn't show much, though, not even when I pointed to Robideaux's atrocity and said, "Nice piece of work here. I was just admiring it."

"Yes. It's quite good, isn't it."

"Local artist?"

"I imagine so. I bought it at a crafts fair a year or so ago. Shall we go out on the deck?"

I considered pushing the topic a little further, maybe coming right out and asking her if she knew Robideaux, but it didn't seem to be the way to handle her. And I'd made enough mistakes by being blunt today as it was. So I shrugged and said, "Sure," and we went out on the deck.

A chaise lounge had been pulled out near the balcony railing, to catch the last of the sun as it passed over to the west; Mrs. O'Daniel sat on that. The only other chair in sight was a Chinese rattan thing with a fanlike back and a narrow seat that looked uncomfortable. And was.

She said, "You're wondering why I wanted to talk to you, of course. It's nothing earthshaking. My husband and I were talking at dinner last night and he mentioned you were here investigating poor Munroe's death for the insurance company, talking to people who knew him, that sort of thing, and that we should all cooperate in any way we can in order to get the matter settled as quickly as possible."

Some sentence. Some Mrs. O'Daniel, too. She had a better reason than that for wanting to see me; and I had a pretty fair idea what it might be. She hadn't had dinner with her husband last night, either, or found out about me that way. He'd reminded her on the phone yesterday that he was leaving from the office for some lake in the area, to spend the weekend on a houseboat.

But I said, "You knew Mr. Randall pretty well, did you?"

"Oh yes. I met him when Frank and I were married several years ago. His death was a terrible shock."

"I'm sure it was."

"Such a tragic accident," she said. She had lowered her voice a couple of octaves and given it a sepulchral tremor; it sounded only about half sincere, like an undertaker sympathizing with somebody else's loss. "That garage of his . . . well, it was an awful firetrap. I don't know how many times Frank and I warned him to clean it up."

I said something noncommittal.

"The police said that's where the fire started—in the garage. Spontaneous combustion. I suppose your findings concur with that?"

"So far they do, yes."

"So far? You mean you think the fire might have started somewhere in the house?"

"I mean it's possible the cause wasn't spontaneous combustion."

She took a large bite out of her gin and tonic; she looked vaguely uneasy now. "I can't imagine what could have caused it then," she said.

"A match, maybe."

"Match? You don't mean arson?"

"It's possible. I haven't ruled it out yet."

"But that's absurd!"

''Your husband doesn't think so. Neither does Martin Treacle.''

''They don't believe the fire was deliberately set.''

''They admitted the possibility.''

''I don't believe it either. It was an accident.''

I waited, not saying anything.

Pretty soon she said, ''Those people in Musket Creek . . . are they the ones you suspect?''

''I don't suspect anyone, Mrs. O'Daniel. Not yet anyhow.'' I paused. ''But it could be one of them; they all seem to have had good reason to hate Randall.''

''I suppose so. I know very little about their problems with Northern Development; I'm not a woman who takes an active interest in her husband's business activities.''

I felt like grinning at her: she just wasn't a very good liar. ''You don't know any of the Musket Creek residents personally, then?''

''Of course not.'' She said it too quickly, seemed to realize that, tried to cover herself by saying something else, and botched that too: ''Why would I have anything to do with anyone who lives in the backwoods?''

''Lots of people live in the backwoods,'' I said. ''Writers, gold hunters, homesteaders. Artists.''

She made the rest of her drink disappear. She didn't look at me while she did it.

Time to back off on that angle, I thought. I asked her, taking a new tack, ''Did your husband tell you about the threatening note he received?''

''Yes, he told me.''

''You don't sound very concerned about it.''

''Why should I be? It was nothing but a crank note, like those telephone calls we kept getting last year. I'm sure Frank mentioned those?''

I nodded. ''And did he also tell you that Jack Coleclaw attacked him in his office yesterday?''

''Well, he said there'd been a minor altercation. But he didn't elaborate.''

''It wasn't so minor. If I hadn't been there, your husband might have been badly hurt.''

She looked at her empty glass, seemed to want to get up and refill it, then just sat there with it in her hand. Her face revealed nothing. Maybe she had a hard shell that was full of feeling on the inside, like a piece of rock candy with a liquid center. Or maybe she just didn't give a damn about her husband's welfare. I thought it was probably the latter; the way it looked to me, the only person Helen O'Daniel cared about was Helen O'Daniel.

I said, "Let's get back to Munroe Randall. I understand he was quite a ladies' man."

She stiffened a little. "What do you mean by that?"

"I was told he had relationships with a lot of different women. Intimate relationships. That's true, isn't it?"

"I . . . yes, I suppose it is."

"Do you know any of his women friends?"

"Not really. I may have met one or two, but . . ."

"How about Penny Belson?"

"That bitch. Munroe should have known better."

"You know Miss Belson, then."

"Yes, I know her. Why? Have you been talking to her?"

"Yesterday at her salon."

"What did she tell you?"

"About what?"

Pause. "She's a liar, you know. And a tramp."

Pot calling the kettle black, I thought.

"What did she say about me?" Mrs. O'Daniel asked.

"Nothing specific. I understand you used to be one of her customers. What happened?"

"I decided to go to another salon, that's all."

"Why? Did you have some sort of trouble with Miss Belson?"

"I don't think that's any of your business."

Time to back off again. "Who else did Randall date regularly?" I asked.

"I told you, I don't really know."

"But you were a friend of his—"

"I didn't pry into his personal life."

"You saw him socially, though, didn't you? Often?"

"Not very often, no."

"Did you see him on the day he died?"

"Of course not." But again she said it too quickly. "I don't see the point of all these questions. Just what are you leading up to?"

"I'm not leading up to anything. I'm only doing my job—asking questions, looking for answers. Trying to find out if anybody has anything to hide."

"Are you insinuating *I* have something to hide?"

"Do you, Mrs. O'Daniel?"

She looked a little pale now under her buttery tan. "No," she said, "I do not," but the lie was there in her eyes, naked and bright. She got to her feet. "I think you'd better leave now," she said coldly. "We have nothing more to say to each other."

"Not for the time being, anyway."

I stood up too, and she turned immediately and led me back through the house to the front entrance. She didn't roll her hips this time; she walked in short, choppy steps with her back stiff and straight. When she got to the door she flung it open, stepped back, and looked at me with her eyes smoldering. Scene in an old-time melodrama, I thought. I half expected her to say something like, "Go, and never darken my door again." But all she said was, "Well?" when I didn't walk out right away.

"Your husband told me he was going to spend the weekend on a houseboat," I said. "I'd appreciate it if you'd tell me where he is."

"Why?"

"Because I want to talk to him again."

"About me, I suppose."

I watched her in silence.

"Oh, all right," she said. "He's at Shasta Lake, at a place called Mountain Harbor."

"Is that a town?"

"No. It's some sort of boat harbor about fifteen miles from here. He keeps his houseboat there."

"*His* houseboat?"

"I don't like boats or water. Now will you please leave?"

I left. And she slammed the door shut behind me.

Up by the platform deck, I paused and took another look at the lemon-colored Porsche with the FAST UN license plate. One of Munroe Randall's neighbors had told me she'd seen "a yellow sports car" parked just down the street from Randall's house some three hours before he and his house went up in flames. It didn't have to have been Helen O'Daniel's Porsche, of course. But I would have given odds and bet a bundle that it was.

Munroe Randall—and maybe Paul Robideaux, too. And no telling yet how many others, or what else she was afraid I might find out about. Helen O'Daniel got around pretty good. For a married woman.

TEN

Three minutes after I pulled into the Sportsman's Rest, Martin Treacle showed up.

I was standing in front of our room, talking to Kerry, when he came wheeling in. She'd been swimming, because the skimpy little white suit she wore was still wet, but her mood wasn't any better than when I'd left her. When I said I was going to drive up to Shasta Lake to see Frank O'Daniel again, and offered to take her along, she said no, she was going to shower and then read: she didn't feel like sitting around and waiting while I conducted any more of my interviews.

Treacle was driving a two-year-old Lincoln Continental. And in spite of the lingering heat he was wearing another three-piece suit, this one made out of some shiny material I didn't recognize. He was one of these people who manage to look cool and comfortable no matter what the temperature, damn him.

He came over and shook my hand in his earnest way. When I introduced him to Kerry he took her hand too, and I thought briefly that the silly bastard was going to kiss it. He let go of it instead and smiled at her in an approving way. She seemed to like that; the smile she gave him in return was warmer than any she'd let me have all day.

Treacle said to me, "I just got in from the city this afternoon. I called Miss Irwin at home and she told me you were staying here."

"Mm."

''How's it going so far?''

''How's what going so far?''

''The investigation,'' he said. ''I guess your findings are about what we expected?''

''Are they?'' I said. ''Maybe not.''

He frowned. ''I don't understand. You mean there's some doubt in your mind about Munroe's death?''

''Some, yes. Did Miss Irwin tell you what happened yesterday at your office?''

''Oh, that,'' Treacle said. ''Yes, she told me. But that couldn't have anything to do with Munroe—''

''Coleclaw committed one act of violence; he could have committed another.''

''But you don't have any evidence of that . . . or do you?''

''Not yet.''

''He's just a crank, that's all,'' Treacle said. ''He probably wrote that threatening letter to Frank too. It doesn't have to mean anything ominous.''

He was annoying me again. I still hadn't managed to work up an active dislike for him, but I was getting closer to it. It wouldn't be long now.

I got the letter out of my wallet and shoved it under his nose. ''Anything familiar about this?'' I asked him. ''The printing, the paper, the style of wording?''

He blinked at the note. Kerry crowded in and peered at it too. I gave her a look, but she didn't pay any attention.

''Well?'' I said to Treacle.

''No,'' he said. ''No, none of it is familiar. It looks like a crank note to me. Doesn't it look that way to you, Miss Wade?''

''Yes,'' she said, ''it does.''

Bah, I thought. I folded the note and put it back into my wallet.

Treacle said, ''Have you been to Musket Creek yet?''

''Yeah, I've been there.''

''What did you find out?''

''Not much from the people I talked to,'' I said. ''But the fire they had was arson.''

''It was?''

''Whoever did it used a candle.'' I went back and opened up the trunk and showed him the cup-shaped piece of stone with the wax residue inside. "I found this among the debris," I said.

He used one of the rags in the trunk to pick it up, and peered at it. Pretty soon he said, "Travertine."

"Huh?"

"That's the kind of mineral this is. Travertine—layered calcium carbonate. Geology is one of my interests."

"An unusual stone?"

"No, not for this part of the country." He rubbed at it with the rag, ridding it of some of the black from the fire. "It's fossilized," he said, and showed me the imprints in the stone. "Bryophytes."

"What are bryophytes?" Kerry asked.

"Nonflowering plants. Mosses and liverworts."

"Is that kind of fossil uncommon?"

"Not really. They turn up fairly often in this area." Treacle picked at the wax residue with his fingernail. "This is purple, isn't it?"

I nodded. "One of the women over there makes purple candles as a hobby. Ella Bloom."

"That one," Treacle said. "She reminds me of a witch."

"Me too. She threatened me with a shotgun when I tried to talk to her."

"My God. What did you do?"

"What would you do if somebody started waving a shotgun at you?"

"Why . . . I'd run, I guess."

"Yeah," I said.

I took the stone away from him, put it back into the trunk, and closed the lid. Kerry was fanning herself with one hand; as late in the day as it was—close to five o'clock—the heat out here was oppressive. Treacle noticed her discomfort and waved a hand toward a restaurant-and-bar that adjoined the motel.

"Why don't we go in where it's cool and have a drink?"

"That's a good idea," Kerry said. "I could use something."

I said, "You want to go into a public place dressed like that?"

"What's wrong with the way I'm dressed?"

"That bathing suit . . ."

"I also happen to be wearing a beach robe," she said. "I'll button it right up to my neck so I won't offend you or anybody else."

"I didn't mean . . . Look, I thought you were going to take a shower and read a book."

"I'd rather have a drink. That is, if you don't mind."

Well, I did mind. I wanted to ask Treacle some personal questions—questions about Munroe Randall and Helen O'Daniel—and I didn't want to do it in front of her because it might inhibit him. But if I told her to leave us alone, I'd pay for it later: I'm not hard-boiled enough, or macho enough, despite Kerry's accusation, to order women around and get away with it. So I sighed—I seemed to be doing a lot of sighing today—and said, "All right." And the three of us went off together to the bar.

Inside, the air conditioner was going full-blast and it was nice and cool. We sat in a booth, away from the half-dozen other patrons, and a waitress came over to take our orders. She was Chinese, and she reminded me vaguely of Jeanne Emerson, and that in turn reminded me of the night Jeanne had come to my flat and what had happened while she was there. The memory made me feel uncomfortable; I couldn't look at Kerry because I was afraid she'd see something in my expression. Some tough guy I was.

So instead I focused my attention on Treacle and launched into an edited version of how things had gone in Musket Creek. When I was done he shook his head in a martyred kind of way and allowed again as how everyone who lived there was a loony. But then he qualified it, for my benefit, by saying that he couldn't believe any of them was really dangerous.

"No?" I said. "How about Jack Coleclaw?"

"Well, anyone can lose his temper, you know. And Frank . . ." He paused because the waitress had returned with our drinks—beer for Kerry and me, a Tom Collins for Treacle. I didn't look at her while she was serving us. "Frank," Treacle continued when she was gone, "well, he's not the most tactful guy in the world."

"He provokes trouble, you mean?"

"No, no. It's just that he's too blunt sometimes. I've tried to tell him you have to be careful when you're dealing with loonies, but he forgets himself."

I started to say something, but before I could get it out Kerry said in miffed tones, "Loonies. Why do you have to keep using that word?"

He blinked at her. "Well, I—"

"They're not such loonies. They only want to be left alone. And they're frustrated." I threw her a warning look but she ignored it. "Mr. Treacle, may I ask you a frank question?"

"Yes, of course."

"Don't you or your partner give a damn what happens to those poor people?"

I felt like reaching across the table and strangling her a little. You don't talk that way to people you're trying to get information out of, people you want to cooperate. At least I don't; if I did I would have ended up unemployed a long time ago. But she got away with it, just as she'd got away with fast-talking Hugh Penrose earlier.

"Certainly we care, Miss Wade," Treacle said. He didn't sound ruffled or defensive; he didn't even sound surprised anymore. Maybe it was a question he'd heard any number of times before. "Neither of us has a heart of stone, you know. And Munroe didn't either."

"Then how can you just waltz into Musket Creek and take their land away from them?"

"We're not trying to take their land away from them," Treacle said patiently. "Why, their own parcels will be worth far more than they are now once we've restored the Gold Rush camp and opened it to the public."

"You mean turned the place into some kind of tourist-trap."

"That's not true. Our plans call for careful, authentic restoration. We're very much interested in improvement and preservation of historical landmarks. . . ."

They went on that way, Kerry offering challenges, Treacle using his salesman's rhetoric to defend himself and his attitudes. She was being controlled now, though, like the leader of a debate team; so was Treacle. I nibbled at my beer and thought how nice it would be to take both of them back to the Sportsman's Rest and throw them into the swimming pool.

What I was waiting for was Kerry to finish her beer. It didn't take her long; she was thirsty and she got it down reasonably fast. When her glass was empty she said, "Excuse me," more to Treacle than to me, and got out of the booth and hurried off. It never fails. The stuff goes right through her; as soon as she takes in twelve ounces, she has to go to the ladies' room. Her plumbing is as predictable as Old Faithful.

Once she was out of earshot I said to Treacle, "I picked up a couple of rumors today. Maybe you can tell me if they're worth anything."

"Rumors?"

"I understand Randall was a ladies' man. One rumor has it that he didn't mind playing around with his friends' wives."

Treacle looked startled. He opened his mouth, shut it again; after about five seconds he said, "Munroe and Helen O'Daniel?"

"Uh-huh."

"Who told you that?"

"A woman named Penny Belson. Is it true?"

"I don't know. My God, how would I know?"

"Randall didn't flaunt his women?"

"No."

"Or talk to you about them?"

"Well, sometimes. But never anything about Helen."

"What about Helen? You think she's a nice, faithful wife or what?"

He hesitated. One hand fumbled inside his coat and came out with a panatela. He started to unwrap it, but then his memory told him I wasn't partial to cigar smoke. He gave me a nervous glance and put the thing away again.

"You didn't answer my question, Mr. Treacle."

He cleared his throat. "Well," he said, "I . . . guess I've heard some things about Helen myself."

"Like what? That she plays around?"

"Yes."

"With anybody you know?"

"No. At least, I don't think so."

"Is O'Daniel aware of what's going on, you think?"

Treacle nodded reluctantly. "He's the one who told me about it."

That startled *me* a little. "He told you his wife sees other men? Why?"

"We were drinking one night at the country club a few months ago. We'd both had a little too much. I don't know, he just started to talk about it."

"Was he upset, angry?"

"No. Just . . . matter-of-fact. He didn't seem to care, particularly. He said it's been going on a long time."

"And he puts up with it? Why doesn't he get a divorce?"

"He can't afford to. He'd have to give Helen half of everything he has. That would mean liquidating assets, selling his house and boat—he just won't do it."

"Okay from his point of view," I said. "But what about hers? Why doesn't *she* get a divorce and take half of everything he's got?"

"I don't know."

"What's your opinion of her? What kind of person do you think she is?"

"I don't really know her very well," he said. "We're not friends."

"She ever make a pass at you?"

"My God, no."

"What would you have done if she had?"

"Turned her down, of course," he said a little stiffly. "Munroe may have played games like that, but I don't."

"Suppose Randall did play games like that. And suppose O'Daniel found out. How do you think he'd have reacted?"

He shook his head. "I can't say."

"How did the two of them get along? Were they friendly?"

"Yes. Of course."

"No friction or anything like that lately?"

"None that I know of." Treacle frowned at me. "You're not trying to suggest that Frank had anything to do with Munroe's death? If you are . . ."

He didn't finish the sentence, and I didn't have to answer his question, because Kerry was coming back from the john. I let her sit down again; then I finished my beer and said, "My turn to be excused. I've got some things to do."

Treacle said, "You're leaving?"

"Yes. I'll be in touch later on. You are planning to stick around Redding for a while, aren't you?"

"Certainly."

Kerry was letting me have one of her looks. "Where are you going?"

"I told you before—up to Shasta Lake for another talk with Frank O'Daniel. You can still come along if you want."

"No. I feel like having another beer."

"Suit yourself." I got out of the booth. "I'll be back in a couple of hours. Then we can have dinner."

She didn't say anything. As far as she was concerned I was already gone. And from the expression on her face she didn't much care when I came back.

ELEVEN

Dusk was just starting to settle when I crossed the bridge over Turntable Bay, at the southern end of the lake. The sun was gone behind the peaks of the Coast Range and the sky in that direction was a dark, smoky red, like old wine. The waterways on both sides of the bridge, dotted with boats and little wooded islets, were glass-smooth and bright with reflections of the dying daylight.

I drove on up Highway 5. On a map, Shasta Lake looks a little like a bony hand with five fingers splayed out toward the north. Hills and heavy forestland obscure parts of it from the highway; they also hide the huge bulk of Shasta Dam, the reason for the lake's existence. Shasta Lake is the largest man-made body of water in the state and has as many miles of shoreline as a year has days. Boating, waterskiing, and fishing are its main attractions. You can get black bass, Kokanee trout, and you don't have to work too hard for the privilege. Just the thought of a Kamloops trout pan-fried in butter made me drool a little. And itch to get this investigation wrapped up so I could hie on out into one of the fingers with my fishing gear.

Mountain Harbor wasn't difficult to find, as it turned out; there was an exit for it right off the freeway. A narrow, switchbacked road took me down a rocky hillside, through a copse of pines, and right up against the lake. There wasn't much to the place. The harbor was small, walled on two sides by high, barren peaks; trees grew in close to the water on the other two sides, giving it a secluded atmosphere. A combination café and store and boat service bulked up to the right of the road, with a couple of log cabins among the pines at the rear.

In front were boat-launching ramps, and alongside those, stretching out into the placid blue-black water, was boat moorage—two rows of floating slips connected by walkways. Maybe a dozen boats were tied up, a fourth or fifth of the number that would crowd it at the height of the summer season. A few were small outboard pleasure craft; the rest were houseboats, the most popular kind of boat on the lake because they gave you all the conveniences of a small housekeeping cabin.

I parked in the lot behind the café. It was cool here, windless because of the sheltering peaks and trees. The sky was yellow-dark now, just a few minutes from nightfall; shadows clung to the trees and the far edges of the harbor, where the lake cut away between a pair of promontories. Lights were on in the café building, and night-lights strung on wire cast pale illumination over the boat slips. There weren't many people around. The only ones I saw were two couples on the aft deck of one of the houseboats—drinking out of tall glasses, talking in mildly sloshed voices, watching night come down.

I skirted the ramps, got onto the floating walkway, and went out toward the boat with the four people on it. None of them paid any attention to me until I came up close to the taffrail and hailed them. Then they all looked at me with a kind of vague disapproval, as if I had interrupted a private communion.

"I'm looking for Frank O'Daniel," I said. "Would you happen to know which boat is his?"

"End slip," one of the men said. "The *Kokanee*."

"Which way?"

He pointed lakeward with the hand holding his glass. Ice clinked, a sound that seemed to carry in the stillness. It was that kind of night.

"Is he on board, do you know?"

"Haven't seen him."

"I saw him," one of the women said. "About an hour ago, over at the store. He was buying a bottle."

"I'll bet you noticed what kind it was, huh, Peg?"

"Dewar's," she said. "White Label. A fifth."

They all thought that was pretty funny. Their laughter rang out among the lengthening shadows, echoing a little before it died.

"He went back to his boat," the woman, Peg, said to me. "Least, I think he did."

"Thanks."

"Welcome, I'm sure." She raised her glass. "Happy New Year," she said.

They all laughed again, and I went around their boat and over onto another walkway. There was only one boat tied up out at the end—a houseboat that looked a little bigger than the others at the moorage. Because of the curve of the shoreline, she was in close to the trees and the rocky promontory that marked the north end of the harbor. The looming pines and the high rock wall threw layers of thick shadow over her.

I walked along to the boat and squinted at the name painted on her vertically flattened stern. *Kokanee.* I stood for a moment looking her over. Except for size, she wasn't much different than any of the others: squarish, with big windows and a wood-slatted superstructure painted white and some dark color that would probably be brown; hull painted the same dark color; railed sundeck on top, railed decks fore and aft. Like a small mobile home outfitted with pontoons and set afloat.

All the windows were dark. She was quiet, too, dead-still in the motionless water. There wasn't anything to hear anywhere except for the half-drunken laughter of the people back at the other houseboat.

Maybe he went out somewhere after all, I thought. But I moved in close to the aft railing and called, "Hello, the *Kokanee*! You on board, Mr. O'Daniel?"

No response.

I called again, identifying myself. Still no answer. Well, what the hell, I thought. If he wasn't here, maybe he'd just gone out for a quick supper and he'd be back pretty soon. I had time on my hands and nothing better to do than wait here a while. It was a nice night and a nice setting for a wait.

So I climbed on board and started aft, lakeward, because I could see some deck chairs set out back there. Only I stopped before I got to the chairs. There was a faint smell in the air that made my nostrils twitch—a familiar, acrid smell. Gasoline.

Something made me call O'Daniel's name again. More silence. No sounds at all on the boat, not even the creak of joints or the mooring ropes; the water was like a sheet of black glass, dappled here and there with moonlight spilling in through the trees.

I went ahead onto the aft deck. The odor was stronger back there—and it shouldn't have been. You shouldn't be able to smell gasoline that strongly on board a moored boat . . .

A bad feeling began to move through me, bunching muscles, building unease. Gasoline-powered marine engines and generators could be dangerous; you have to be careful around them. I didn't know much about boats but I knew that much.

Where the hell was O'Daniel?

I hesitated. Part of me wanted to go on inside, take a look around; part of me wanted to get off this boat in a hurry, away from those gas fumes. I took a couple of steps without really making up my mind, on my way to do one or the other.

A sudden muffled ringing noise started up inside the cabin.

My scalp prickled and I stopped again. The sound continued, still steady and muffled; I couldn't identify what it was. Was somebody in there or not? Somebody doing something in the dark?

I yelled, "Hey! Hello inside!" Still no response, except for that insistent jangling.

The feeling of unease was acute now; so was the desire to get off this boat. In my mind there was a confused thought of gasoline leakage and bilges and fumes gathering and the danger of a single spark from an electrical switch. I started to run for the rail, to vault over onto the walkway.

Muffled popping sound, then a kind of faint whooshing.

Flash of blinding light, thunderous concussion—

—wild terror—

—moment of blackness—

—and I was in the water, black and bright orange water full of floating things. Thrashing around in the water, gagging, choking, with it cold in my mouth and throat. A roaring in my ears, light and heat beating against me. I went under, fought back up, and then the wildness and the disorientation cleared out of my head and I could think again. I kicked my body around to face into the heat and the glare.

The *Kokanee* was sheeted with fire, flames reaching up like trembly hands into the black sky. People were running along the shore and the floats. Yelling, too, but it was all a long way off, like hearing something through a wall.

An awareness of pain worked its way into my mind. Burning pain, burns—my face and arms were burned. Men were out on one of the floats now, silhouetted against the glow of the fire, one of them waving his arms and shouting orders to the others; two or three more were extending a long metal gaff out into the water in my direction. I started to swim, hurting, frightened, but functioning all right—not burned too badly to swim all right.

Debris bobbed all around me. I pushed through it toward the gaff. Something struck my cheek, something pliable, and I saw what it was and gagged again and batted it away with a little of the wildness coming back.

It was somebody's blown-off arm.

TWELVE

They started hammering questions at me as soon as they pulled me out of the water. *What happened are you all right where's Frank O'Daniel was it the fuel tank was there anybody else on board*—a babble of words that seemed to rise and fall with the thrumming of the fire. Their faces were surreal masks of light and shadow, like participants in some sort of pagan ceremony. I shook my head at them, pushed their hands away. Stood there dripping: I wasn't going to fall down.

"Call the sheriff." The words came out all loose and funny, as if something had been broken or knocked out of kilter in my throat. "Somebody's been killed."

Buzz, buzz, thrum and buzz: *Who was killed was it Frank God A'mighty I thought I saw something out there looked like an arm . . .*

"Call the sheriff, will you? Call the sheriff!"

"Already been done, mister," somebody said. It was the guy who had been shouting orders. "My wife's taken care of it. They're on the way."

I said, "Okay," and shoved past him, went away from all of

them. I could walk all right, but my knees were wobbly and I took slow, careful steps, like a drunk trying to walk a straight line. In the firelight I could see that my clothing was scorched and waterlogged, hanging on me like strips of peeled skin. My face hurt; so did my hands, my arms. But it wasn't that intolerable kind of fiery pain you feel when you've been badly burned. I touched my cheek: hot and wet and sore, but not raw, not blistered. Lucky. Jesus, I was lucky—that arm out there could have been mine. . . .

There was a boat nearby, a small runabout, probably an outboard, with a tarp stretched over it and tied down. I sat on its gunwale and looked at the *Kokanee.* Not much left of it now. A floating pyre canted over to one side, lying low in the water, flames shooting through a gaping hole the explosion had ripped in its superstructure. Three guys with buckets were busy scooping water over the board floats down there, to make sure the fire didn't spread to the rest of the boats. That was what the other guy, the one whose wife had telephoned the sheriff, had been shouting about while I was still in the lake. There wasn't much else for anybody to do. You couldn't even hope to put out a fire like that with a bucket brigade.

The take-charge guy came over to where I was sitting, the boozer I'd talked to earlier dogging along behind him. "You'd better come to my cabin," he said, "get out of those wet clothes, get some salve on your burns." He sounded pretty calm, as if boats blowing up and people getting killed were commonplace things to him. "I'll call you a doctor."

"Who're you?"

"Tom Decker. I own the facilities here."

The boozer said, "How could a thing like that happen? How the hell can a boat just blow up like that?"

"If you knew anything about boats, Les," Decker said mildly, "you wouldn't have to ask that question."

"What kind of crack is that? I know plenty about boats."

"Sure you do." Decker shifted his gaze to me again. "If you don't think you can make it under your own steam . . ."

"No, I'm okay. Not that badly hurt."

He nodded. "But you don't want to let burns go untreated," he said. "Come on with me."

I stood up again, giving the *Kokanee* another look. It would burn right down to the waterline in another few minutes, I thought. The sheriff's people would probably have to drag for what was left of O'Daniel's body. If it *was* O'Daniel whose arm was out there in the dark water.

I went with Decker, leaving the other guy, Les, to puzzle out the explosion by himself. Decker's cabin was one of those in back and to one side of the café-and-store, and a slim, dark-haired woman was waiting in the doorway. He introduced her as his wife, Mary or Marie. Inside, they pointed me into the kitchen and Decker went and got some towels and an old bathrobe while she examined my face and arms. When he came back she disappeared, and I took the opportunity to shuck out of my wet clothing and dry off and bundle up in the robe.

Decker said, "Looks like your burns are superficial. But I'm going to call a doctor anyway."

"Why?"

"You can never tell about burns. I've seen enough cases to know that they ought to be looked after right away by a competent medic."

I studied him a little. He was about forty-five, lean, brown, with a long sad face and eyes that said he had stopped being excited about things a long time ago; eyes that had known pain. I had seen eyes like that before.

"Ex-military?" I asked him. "Vietnam?"

"Yes. I've got the look, right?"

"You've got the look."

"You've got one too," he said. "Police officer?"

"Private detective. I'm investigating the death of Frank O'Daniel's partner, for their insurance company."

He raised a questioning eyebrow. "Was O'Daniel on board the *Kokanee* when she blew?"

"Somebody was. He's the most likely."

"I read about the fire that killed Randall; O'Daniel talked about it some himself. Now this. Coincidence?"

I didn't say anything. I was thinking: Two fatal "accidents" involving fire; two partners dying within a week of each other. Coincidence? Not too damned likely.

Decker's wife came back with a tube of pinkish gunk and began to smooth the stuff over my face and the reddened surface of my arms and hands. It took most of the pain away instantly. Decker went to make another telephone call—presumably the doctor he'd mentioned. Through the cabin window I could see that the fire had died down some already: the orange stain had begun to fade out of the night.

When Decker rejoined us he said, "Doctor'll be here in fifteen minutes or so." I nodded, and he asked, "You want to talk about what happened out there?"

"I don't know what happened, exactly. Maybe you can tell me." I went on to explain how it had been: the smell of gasoline, the jangling noise, the pop and whoosh and the sudden explosion that had followed almost immediately.

He was frowning when I finished. "Doesn't make much sense," he said. "That ringing you heard—could it have been the telephone? O'Daniel had one of those battery-powered jobs—"

"No," I said. "it wasn't that kind of noise. Steady, no breaks in it."

He shook his head. "I can't think of anything he might've been doing that accounts for it. Or for those gas fumes. The man had plenty of faults but he was a good sailor. He knew boats."

"Did he drink heavily?" I asked. "One of the people outside told me he bought a bottle earlier tonight."

"Well, he drank more than some."

"Did you sell him the bottle?"

"Yes. He'd had a couple of drinks but he wasn't drunk."

"That was about an hour before the explosion?"

"About."

"How did he seem to you? What was his mood?"

"Cheerful. He seemed normal enough."

"Was he alone when he came in?"

"Yes."

"And alone on his boat today?"

"As far as I know." He looked at his wife. "Marie?"

"I didn't see him with anyone," she said.

I asked, "Did he have any visitors this weekend?"

"Not that I saw," she said, and Decker shook his head. "But we don't pay much attention to what our renters do, as long as they don't bother others."

"Did he ever come here with anyone?"

"He used to bring his wife, but he hasn't done that in a while."

Decker said, "Drunk or sober, why didn't he smell the gasoline and do something about it? That's what I'm wondering."

"Me too," I said. "What about the explosion? Does that sort of thing happen often?"

"It happens, but not usually with houseboats like the *Kokanee.*" He paused speculatively. "Still, she shouldn't have made a boom like that. Shouldn't have burned that hot, either."

"What do you mean?"

"That was a hell of a big boom," he said. "There shouldn't have been enough gasoline or other flammables on board to blow with that much force. Or to make her burn as hot and fast as she did."

"I see."

"O'Daniel could have stored up flammables for some reason of his own," Decker said. "People aren't very bright sometimes. But it's not likely."

We looked at each other. I said, "Suppose it was no accident. Can you fit the facts into an explanation?"

"Sure, if it was suicide. But that's a hell of a way to knock yourself off. And why would he want to take you with him?"

"No reason I can think of," I said. "How about if it also wasn't suicide? How about if it was murder?"

He spread his hands. "I can add up part of it that way, not all of it. Maybe I'm just slow, but I don't see how it *could* be murder."

"I must be slow too," I said. "Neither do I."

Two cars full of county sheriff's deputies, and a fat and dour plainclothes investigator named Telford, showed up before long. So did the doctor Decker had called. Telford asked me questions while the doctor examined me and the deputies prowled around outside. Rehashing my account of things didn't open up any new insights; nor did anything come out of the deputies' questioning of the other Mountain Harbor renters. Nobody had seen or heard anything suspicious prior to the explosion, and nobody had any other information that might explain what had happened.

The doctor confirmed Decker's and my opinion that my burns were superficial, and decided that the pinkish stuff Mrs. Decker had spread on me was all the medication I required. Telford decided my soggy identification was genuine, and that I had no apparent sinister motives, and could be released on my own recognizance. Come in to his office in Redding tomorrow and make a formal statement, he said. Good-bye, he said.

There wasn't any reason for me to hang around there any longer; they weren't going to get what was left of Frank O'Daniel out of the *Kokanee* for a while yet, maybe not until morning, and even if they did I had no desire to watch them do it. I borrowed an old pair of pants and a shirt from Decker, thanked him and his wife, bundled up my own stuff, and got out of there.

When I came into Kerry's and my room at the Sportsman's Rest it was after ten o'clock. She was lying on the bed reading a mystery novel by somebody named Muller. She took one look at me, made startled noises, threw the book aside, bounced off the bed, and said, "For God's sake, what happened to you?" in a half-concerned, half-frightened voice—a reaction that made me feel loved again.

I told her what had happened to me. She didn't like it; she never likes it when I have a brush with violence—not that I'm keen on it myself. But she settled down after a time and put her arms around me, and that was good in more ways than one because it meant she was over her pique and we were going to get on again. For a while, anyway.

I got a couple of minutes of cuddling. Then she let go of me and gave me a critical look, and a small smile played at the corners of her mouth. "Well," she said, "at least one good thing came out of tonight."

"Yeah? What's that?"

"Go look in the mirror."

I went into the bathroom and looked in the mirror. My face was mottled, still lobster-red in patches across both cheeks, greasy with Mrs. Decker's pink gunk. And my upper lip was more or less naked.

"You see?" Kerry said from the doorway. "The explosion did what I've been yearning to do for weeks. It singed that stupid mustache right off."

THIRTEEN

Frank O'Daniel was the person who'd died in the explosion, all right; I got the word on that Sunday morning, when I went to the sheriff's office in Redding to keep my promise to Telford. O'Daniel had been the only casualty. They'd found his charred remains in the *Kokanee's* cockpit—and his blown-off arm floating around among the debris in the lake—and they had identified him through his dental charts. An autopsy had been performed, but nothing had come of that—no indications of foul play.

"I don't see how the coroner can stand his job," Telford said. He shook his head, leaned back in his desk chair, and belched dyspeptically. "Must have been like trying to autopsy a piece of overcooked steak."

Nice analogy, I thought. But I said, "Yeah, I guess. Have you notified Mrs. O'Daniel yet?"

"I just got back from talking to her a few minutes ago."

"How did she take it?"

He grimaced. "The way they usually take it. Cried some and carried on."

"Like he was the love of her life, huh? Like she can't bear the thought of going on without him?"

"More or less." Now he was frowning. "What're you getting at?"

"It wasn't that way between them," I said, and I told him the things I'd found out about Helen O'Daniel and the other things I suspected—an affair with Munroe Randall, perhaps another one with Paul Robideaux.

Telford gave that some thought. Then he belched again, said ruefully, "My wife made a Spanish omelette with hot sauce for breakfast," unwrapped a Rolaids tablet, chewed and swallowed it, and said, "You don't think what happened at Mountain Harbor was an accident?"

"Let's just say I'm suspicious. How does it look to you?"

"Suspicious," he said, "but not enough to get me excited about it—yet. No evidence so far that says it was anything but an accident. Or *how* it could've been anything but an accident."

"But you're still working on it?"

"Oh, we're real tenacious types up here in the sticks," he said mildly. "We're not too smart, but once we get our teeth into something we just don't like to let go."

"I'm like that too," I said without missing a beat. "It's a good way for a detective to be."

That was the right thing to say, for a change; maybe this was going to be a better day than the last one—as long as I paid more attention to what came out of my fat mouth. Telford made a sound that was half grunt and half belch and said, "Yeah, it is. Well, I've been in touch with Hank Betters, over at the police department. He thinks two business partners dying in odd accidents within a week of each other is suspicious, same as you and I do. But there's also no evidence of foul play in the Munroe Randall case; you know that. Until some evidence turns up, on one case or the other—*if* it does—there's no use in any of us getting excited. You agree?"

"I agree. But I'd like to keep poking around on my own, if you don't mind."

"Why should I mind? You've got a good rep—I checked you out last night—and there's no reason you shouldn't keep on working."

"Thanks."

"For what? I'm always grateful for a little help from a big-city investigator."

"Put the needle away, okay? I don't think you're a hick."

He grinned a little and ate another antacid tablet. "Suppose both Randall and O'Daniel *were* murdered," he said. "Who do you figure for it? O'Daniel's wife?"

"Well, she might be mixed up in it. She's got plenty of motive."

"So does the surviving partner."

"Treacle's also the most obvious suspect. He'd have to be pretty stupid."

"Maybe he is," Telford said. "All murderers are stupid, especially the ones that try to be clever."

"You talk to him yet?"

"On the phone. He's on his way down."

''How did *he* take the news?''

''Seemed pretty shaken up. We'll see when he gets here. Who else has motive, far as you know?''

''The artist, Robideaux, for one.''

''*If* he was involved with Mrs. O'Daniel.''

''Even if he wasn't,'' I said.

''You mean the hassle between Northern Development and the people in Musket Creek? Yeah, that's another angle.''

''The best one of all, maybe.''

I got out the threatening letter Frank O'Daniel had received. It had been in my wallet and had suffered some water damage last night, but it was still intact and the printing on it was still legible. I passed it over to Telford, explaining what it was and where I'd got it. I also apologized for not having remembered it last night—not that the oversight mattered much. None of us had known for sure then that O'Daniel was the victim.

He said after he'd scrutinized it, ''If this is the McCoy, you could be right about Musket Creek being the best angle. The only thing is . . .'' He tapped the letter with his fingernail. ''Did Randall receive anything like this before he died?''

''Not that anybody claims to know about.''

''Any other kind of threat?''

''Apparently not.''

''Then how come O'Daniel got one? Assuming both men were murdered, why put O'Daniel on his guard with a note? Why not just blow him up?''

''You said it yourself: murderers are stupid.''

''Mm.''

''Could be, too, that the note was sent by somebody else in Musket Creek—a crank thing. Both Treacle and O'Daniel told me they were harassed a while back by hang-up telephone calls. This fits the same pattern. There doesn't *have* to be a connection between the letter and O'Daniel's death.''

Telford ruminated in silence.

''Another thing,'' I said. ''The note didn't put O'Daniel on his guard. He shrugged it off as crank stuff.''

''He did, huh?''

''He also shrugged off something else,'' I said, and I told him about Jack Coleclaw's attack on O'Daniel at the Northern offices and how I'd managed to break it up.

"I think I'd better have a talk with Coleclaw," Telford said. "As soon as I get done with Treacle."

"I think I'll see what I can find out about Mrs. O'Daniel and Paul Robideaux. Unless you have any objections . . ."

"Be my guest. Just be sure to let me know if you find out anything."

"First thing." I got on my feet.

Telford said, "Those burns hurting you much?"

"Some. Why?"

"The way you move. Your face looks raw too."

"It doesn't feel as bad as it looks," I said. But I was aware of the dull ache again, now that he'd called my attention to it.

"If I were you," he said, "I'd wear a hat outdoors. And stay out of direct sunlight."

I took my old shapeless fisherman's hat out of my back pocket and showed it to him. "I already thought of that."

"Smart guy," he said, but there was no irony in his voice. He was eating another Rolaids and grimacing when I walked out of his office.

I went across the outer lobby, past a morose-looking guy who was explaining to a deputy that he *hadn't* been poaching, the damned doe had been shot by somebody else and had staggered over to where he was camped and what the hell was he going to do, let all that good meat just lie there and rot? It was an interesting story but the deputy wasn't buying it; I wouldn't have bought it either, in his place.

Heat slapped at me when I stepped outside, making my face and hands burn dully. I put the hat on so that it drooped down over the upper half of my face. There wasn't much direct sunlight to worry about; you couldn't see the sun at all at the moment. Clouds had begun piling up sometime during the night and there were thunderheads obscuring Mt. Shasta to the east. Storm building. Which was fine by me; maybe it would cool things off.

I started down the front steps. A big, paunchy man was coming along the walk from the parking area; he stopped when he saw me and stood there. I recognized him at just about the same time.

Jack Coleclaw.

He waited, stolidly, for me to get to where he was. Then he said,

"You're the fellow in O'Daniel's office the other night."

"The one who broke up the trouble—that's right."

"Insurance detective," he said, as if the words were a pair of obscenities.

I just looked at him. He seemed nervous, ill-at-ease. And worried. It was hot, but it wasn't hot enough to make a man sweat the way he was sweating.

"I never meant to hurt him, mister," he said. "I just . . . I lost my head for a minute, that's all. I wouldn't of choked the life out of him, even if you hadn't come in. I'm not a killer."

"Tell that to Jim Telford, Mr. Coleclaw."

"Who?"

"Sheriff's investigator in charge of the O'Daniel case. You've heard what happened to Frank O'Daniel, haven't you?"

"Yeah, I heard," Coleclaw said. "On the radio in my truck a little while ago. That's why I'm here—I figured they'd want to talk to me, even if it was an accident."

"Was it?" I said.

He wiped sweat off his face with one of his big paws. "You trying to say it wasn't?"

"No. I'm saying it might not have been."

"What, then? Somebody blew that boat up some way?"

"That's a possibility."

"Well, what does this Telford think?"

"Ask him yourself; he'll tell you."

"No, listen, I'm asking you. He don't think I had anything to do with it, does he?"

"Did you, Mr. Coleclaw?"

"No! Christ, no. I wasn't anywhere near Shasta Lake last night. I was home and I can prove it. My kid was there with me."

"Like I said—tell that to Jim Telford."

"Okay. But I'm telling you too. I didn't have anything to do with O'Daniel getting killed and I didn't have anything to do with Randall getting killed either. I was home with my son that night too."

I had nothing to say.

"Nobody in Musket Creek had anything to do with them two dying," he said. "You understand? Nobody!" He wiped his face again, hunched his shoulders, and stepped around me and went away up the steps.

I watched after him until the building swallowed his bulk, thinking: Funny bird—what yanks his chain for him, anyway? I couldn't decide whether or not he was dangerous; I couldn't get much of a handle on him at all. Well, maybe Telford could. Or maybe there just wasn't much of a handle to get hold of in the first place. I shrugged and swung around and started over toward the parking lot.

And Martin Treacle's Continental was there, just skidding into one of the diagonal slots nearby. Treacle was behind the wheel, and he had two passengers. One, I saw as they got out, was the secretary, Shirley Irwin. The other, for some reason, was Kerry.

FOURTEEN

Treacle was in a dither. His face was pale, his hands twitched, his eyes kept doing odd little flicks and rolls, as if he were about to go into some kind of fit, and he had a slight stutter when he spoke. He came charging over to me and said, "Why didn't you call me last night? For God's sake, why didn't you tell—*tell* me what happened?"

"Take it easy, Mr. Treacle. I didn't call you because I didn't want to sound a false alarm; nobody was sure yet it was your partner who died in the explosion."

"You should have notified me anyway. I had a right—a right to know, didn't I?"

Kerry and Miss Irwin made us a not very appealing foursome. The secretary didn't seem cool and efficient this morning; she looked distraught in a contained sort of way. Kerry's face was almost as pale as Treacle's, as if she'd had some kind of shock or scare herself.

I said to her, "This is a surprise. What're you doing here?"

But Treacle didn't give her a chance to answer; he said, still nattering, "We went to your motel after the sheriff—the sheriff's man called. I wanted to talk to you first, before I see him."

"Why?"

"You were there last night, you almost got killed yourself. It wasn't an accident, was it?"

"That's what everybody wants to know. The exact cause of the explosion hasn't been determined yet."

"But it must have been an accident," Miss Irwin said. "Fuel leaked into the bilges and some kind of spark set it off—that's what the radio said. Poor Frank must have forgotten to use the blowers."

"Maybe."

"There *is* some doubt, then?"

"A reasonable amount."

"Did someone see something, is that it?"

"No. It's nothing specific."

Treacle said, "It's murder, all right. Somebody killed Frank—killed Munroe, too, we were wrong about that. And now I'm—now I'm next in line."

He'd changed his tune completely. Neither Northern Development nor all that insurance money—at least $200,000 now—appeared to matter much to him anymore; what he was worried about at the moment was his own hide. Or so it seemed. The fear looked genuine enough, but you can't be sure about things like that. It could all be an act, a smokescreen, designed to divert suspicion from himself.

"They want me dead," he was saying now, "all those people in Musket Creek. Coleclaw, that son of a bitch, there's one for sure." He leaned my way and poked me in the chest with a forefinger. "You were talking to him when we drove in. What were you talking about?"

I resisted an impulse to slap his hand away. Whether he was putting on an act or not, I had finally reached the point where I could dislike him. Actively, if not with any particular malice. I said, "Nothing that concerns you, Mr. Treacle."

"Why is he here? He didn't come—come to turn himself in, did he?"

"No. He's here because of the fight he had with O'Daniel on Friday evening. He knows it makes him look bad—"

"You're goddamn—damn right it does."

"But he says he has an alibi for last night. And an alibi for the night of Munroe Randall's death. If those alibis stand up he's in the clear."

"All right, so maybe it wasn't him. Maybe it wasn't. But somebody out there is a mur—a murderer. And you better find out who he is. You or Telford or some—*somebody.*"

I kept my mouth shut.

"I'm going to demand police protection," he said. "I'm going to tell—tell Telf—tell Tel—*shit*! Look at me, I'm a nervous—nervous wreck, I can't even talk straight."

Miss Irwin took his arm. "We'd better go inside," she said. He started to resist, but she held on and said in one of those calm, stern voices mothers use on their troublesome kids, "This isn't doing any of us any good. Come on, now."

"All right," he said, "all right." He let her lead him away about three paces, but then he twisted his head around and said to me, "You just find out who kill—who killed Frank and Munroe, that's all. You just find out."

"Sure," I said to shut him up, "I'll find out."

They moved off. Kerry stayed where she was, and when they were out of earshot she said, "I hope Ms. Irwin's got enough sense to do the driving when they leave. God, he drove like a maniac on the way over here from the motel."

"Is that why you were so pale when you got out?"

"You'd have been pale too. He almost hit a bus, two pedestrians, and a motorcycle. I thought I was going to wet my pants."

"What's she doing with him anyway? It's Sunday."

"She lives near him; he stopped and picked her up on the way in. For moral support, I guess."

"Why did *you* come along?"

"I was bored. And you said you'd be here." She pulled a rueful face. "But if I'd known he was going to drive like that I'd have walked."

"You must have seen how upset he is. You could have figured it out from that."

"We can't all have great deductive minds like yours, you know," she said. "Not that I'm incapable of a deduction or two myself. I'd make a pretty good detective if I set my mind to it."

"Sure you would."

"You don't think so?"

"I just said you would. How about if we get out of this heat? My face hurts a little."

"Poor baby. Maybe you should put some more salve on it."

"Good idea."

We went over to my car and got in. Kerry said, "Where to now? Back to the motel?"

"Yup. For the salve, plus I've got to call Barney Rivera."

"And then?"

"Out to Mountain Harbor to return the clothes I borrowed from Tom Decker last night."

"I'd like to see that place," she said. "I'll keep you company."

I didn't see any reason why she shouldn't, so I said, "All right," and started the car.

Barney was home, probably shacked up with a blonde from his office for the weekend; his voice had that satisfied, well-fed tone when he first came on the line. But it didn't last long. He made a wounded noise when I told him about Frank O'Daniel's death and started grumbling at me, as if the whole thing was my fault and I was head of a conspiracy to make his life difficult.

I let him get away with that for a time; then I said, "Listen, Barney, there's a hell of a lot more going on up here than you led me to believe. I can't help it if things keep happening."

"Is there any chance it's murder? Hell, it *must* be murder. I don't buy that kind of coincidence."

"Neither do I. But there's no evidence so far."

"The directors are going to scream if we have to pay off twice on that goddamn double indemnity clause. What about the surviving partner? Treacle? If he killed them for the money we won't have to pay him a dime."

"If he killed them. And if it can be proved."

"Concentrate on him," Barney said. "Come down hard on him if you have to. Let's get this thing resolved fast."

"Screw you, Barney," I said.

"What?"

"I'll call you again when I've got something to report," and I hung up on him just as he began to squawk.

On the way up Highway 5, Kerry and I talked about the two apparently unrelated and accidental deaths; the people who might be involved if the deaths turned out not to be accidental after all. She seemed fascinated, as she often was by my investigations, and her questions and comments were sharp. A very intelligent lady, my lady, even if she did drive me nuts sometimes.

There were more than a few cars on the switchbacked road leading down to Mountain Harbor, and a hell of a lot of people milling around along the lakefront when we got there. Curiosity seekers, drawn by the news of tragedy and sudden death; vultures hunting for scraps of the lurid and the sensational to help sustain their meager lives. What they were feeding on at the moment was the activity of half a dozen men, a couple of them sheriff's deputies, who were winching the fire-gutted wreckage of the *Kokanee* out of the lake.

Thunder grumbled overhead as Kerry and I made our way to the café-and-store; black and bloated clouds moved restlessly above the high rock walls protecting the harbor. The sound of the winch made a whining, ratchey counterpoint to the thunder, and the two sounds together put little cold skitterings on my back. The water had a dull black shine and looked too-still—like something waiting. I had a clear mental image of the way it had been last night, out there in that black water, swimming through the debris with O'Daniel's blown-off arm touching my face. And I shivered a little and looked away.

Tom Decker and his wife were both inside the store; I'd expected to find them either there or in their own cabin—somewhere away from that eager crowd outside. I introduced Kerry to them, and returned the bundle of borrowed clothing.

Decker said, "I've been giving some thought to what we talked about last night—you know, the possibility that O'Daniel's boat was deliberately blown up. I still can't figure a way it could've been done, not unless he arranged it himself to commit suicide."

"I don't think that's likely," I said. "It has to be either an accident or murder."

"Which way are you leaning?"

"Away from accident. But that's not based on anything substantial yet."

"Well, if you're right," he said, "it has to have been some sort of rigged-up device, something that would cause the explosion without the killer being on board and without leaving any traces. If somebody else thought of it, one of us ought to be able to think of it too, sooner or later."

When we went outside again the sheriff's men had the *Kokanee* winched clear and were getting ready to load it onto a long boat trailer. I drove us away from there without wasting any time. I did not want to look at that dripping, burned-out hulk; I wanted to forget it and last night as quickly as possible, bury them in that shallow mental grave I reserved for the horrors and near-horrors that touched my life.

The first drops of rain began to splatter against the windshield just after we turned onto Highway 5. Within minutes, it was coming down in sheets and the gusty wind that had sprung up with it was strong enough to wobble the car. Lightning slashed and flickered in the vicinity of Mt. Shasta. Thunder kept rumbling, very close, very loud. The day turned so dark it was almost like dusk, and what light remained was a wet, eerie gray, tinged with yellow every now and then from the lightning flashes.

Neither of us said much until we crossed the bridge over Turntable Bay. Then Kerry asked, "Where are we going now?" She sounded a little subdued; I thought it was probably the weather. It made me feel a little subdued myself.

"*We're* not going anywhere," I said. "You're going back to the motel; I'm going to Musket Creek."

"Oh? And why don't I get to go there too?"

"Because I'm going to see Paul Robideaux and it might not be a pleasant discussion. Besides which, you coming along yesterday didn't work out too well."

"Meaning I got in your way, I suppose."

"Meaning it might not be safe for you out there."

"Oh, crap," she said. "You still won't admit you handled things badly yesterday, will you?"

"All right, I'll admit it. But that was yesterday; this is today. And another man died in between. I'm going alone—that's all there is to it."

I expected her to give me more argument, the you're-a-macho-jerk routine again, but she didn't. "Do what you have to," she said, and scrunched down on the seat, and sat staring out at the rain. She didn't have anything else to say on the ride to Sportsman's Rest, and nothing to say once we got there; she just opened the door and got out of the car and ran for the room.

Another fun evening ahead, I thought gloomily as I U-turned out of the motel lot. Some job. Some vacation. Some soul mate.

It was enough to make you consider misogyny as an alternative lifestyle.

FIFTEEN

There was rain at Musket Creek too, but it wasn't as heavy, and little jigsaw patterns of blue were visible here and there among the clouds. The lightning and all but dim echoes of the thunder had stayed over near Redding. In the dreary light, the little valley and its collection of relics and anomalies had a desolate, forgotten look, like a vision of something out of the past—something small and insignificant, something doomed.

The road was muddy from the rain; I had had to drive at twenty all the way in from Highway 299, and had to crawl at an even slower pace down the steep hillside into town. Lights burned in Coleclaw's mercantile, in Ella Bloom's cottage up on the hillock—pale blobs against the wet gray afternoon—but nobody was out and around that I could see. I drove in among the ghosts of Ragged-Ass Gulch. My imagination made them into crouching things, battered and weary old shades with blind eyes and signboards for mouths, waiting for night to fall. The things they'd seen, the things they knew . . . just the thought of it put a small, cold ruffling on the back of my scalp, as if somebody had blown his breath across it.

I saw no one among the buildings either, and no one on the way up the far slope and into the woods. The shadows were thick here; it might have been twilight. The rain made hollow dripping noises in the trees, glistened and writhed like silverfish in my headlight beams.

Paul Robideaux's cabin was just that—a country cabin made out of notched logs, with a peaked roof to keep the snow from piling up during the winter. Both front windows showed light. Down in front, just off the road, was the jeep Robideaux had been driving yesterday.

It was alone there, until I put my car alongside it and gave it some company.

Robideaux must have heard the sound of my car's engine; the front door opened just as I reached the porch and he stood there glowering at me. The glower faded somewhat when he got a good look at my face, but he pumped it up again after a couple of seconds and said, "What the hell are you doing here?" in the same belligerent tone he'd used on our first meeting.

"I've got some questions to ask you, Mr. Robideaux."

"You tried that yesterday," he said. "It didn't work then; it's not going to work now. Beat it. I've got nothing to say to you."

"Maybe you'll have something to say to the county sheriff's investigators, then."

"What?"

"They'll be along pretty soon. And they won't be as easy to deal with as I am."

"I don't know what you're talking about."

"No? I'm talking about Frank O'Daniel."

"That bastard. What about him?"

"He's dead. Or didn't you know?"

It seemed he hadn't known. Either that, or he was putting on a good act. He said, "Dead? What do you mean, dead?"

"It's been on the radio."

"I don't listen to the radio. O'Daniel . . . what happened to him? How did he die?"

"His houseboat blew up last night at Shasta Lake. I was there; I almost got blown up myself."

"Jesus," Robideaux said. The belligerence was gone now; he looked shaken, a little pale around the gills.

"It might have been an accident," I said, "just like Munroe Randall's death might have been an accident. I'm betting neither one was, though. I'm betting they were both murdered."

He shook his head, as if he were only half listening to me; the other half of his mind seemed to be on something else. "I don't know anything about it," he said. "I was here last night."

"Alone?"

"Yes. Alone."

"No visitors?"

''Listen, you,'' he said, ''I'm not doing any more talking. Not to you, not to anybody until I see my lawyer.'' He started to back up, to close the door.

I said, ''Have it your way. I'll go get the truth out of Mrs. O'Daniel.''

He stopped backing. ''What's that supposed to mean?''

''What do you think it means?''

''You tell me, smart-ass.''

''I've seen that painting of yours she'd got hanging over her fireplace,'' I said. ''And I know about the two of you. Now you and I can talk it over, or I can go to her. Either way. And watch what you call me from now on. I've had all the crap I'm going to take off you or anybody else.''

Part of it was a shot in the dark; if there was nothing between him and Helen O'Daniel, all he had to do was slam the door in my face. But he didn't do that. He just stood there looking at me. No glower now; his long, thin face was still pale, and if anything he looked worried and maybe a little scared.

Ten seconds went by while we matched stares. It was no contest, though: He let his breath out in a wobbly sigh and said, ''Okay. We'll talk.''

''Inside, huh? It's wet out here.''

He backed up again, into the room this time, and let me come in and shut the door. The place was as much an artist's studio as it was living quarters; most of the rear wall was glass, a skylight had been cut into the roof back there, and that part of the room was cluttered with easels, canvases, a table full of bottles and tubes and brushes, a paint-stained drop cloth on the floor. The walls were covered with finished oils, and more were propped up along the baseboard—fifty or sixty altogether, at a quick guess. Not all of them were as awful as the one over Helen O'Daniel's fireplace, but they were all in the same vomit-stirred-on-canvas class and all done in odd pastels and off-colors. The effect was almost hallucinatory, like a bad trip on some drug or other. A claustrophobe trapped in here would have gone bonkers inside of ten minutes.

Robideaux had entered a little kitchen alcove and was rummaging in a cupboard. He came out with a bottle of bourbon, poured himself about three fingers, downed them in one swallow. Then he shuddered and walked back to where I was. There was color in his cheeks now, the same shade as his fiery hair; he seemed to have himself under a kind of rigid control.

He said, "How did you find out about Helen and me?"

"I'm a detective, remember?"

"Yeah, well, it's not as bad as it looks."

"No?"

"No. They were going to get a divorce."

"Were they? That's news to me."

"It's the truth. So you see? Neither of us had any reason to kill O'Daniel."

"Sure. Except that now she gets *all* their assets, not just half of them."

"I don't like the way your dirty little mind works," he said.

"I could say the same thing about yours, if you want to play it that way."

We glared at each other some more. It was no contest this time, either; he turned abruptly and went to an easy chair covered in brown cloth and folded his big frame into it stiffly. He sat there not looking at me.

I moved over near him, but I stayed on my feet. "How long have you and Mrs. O'Daniel been seeing each other?"

"Don't you know? I thought you knew everything."

"Some things, not all. That's why I'm here."

Pretty soon he said, "All right. About three months."

"Regularly?"

"Whenever we could. Two or three times a week."

"Out here?"

"No. Her place sometimes, during the day. Motels."

"How did you meet her?"

"She showed up at a crafts fair in Red Bluff, where I had some of my paintings on exhibit. We got to talking and we hit it off." He shrugged. "So we ended up back here."

"Didn't she have any qualms about coming to Musket Creek?"

"Later, sure. Not that night."

"Why not?"

"She didn't know who I was or where I lived until we got here; she never involved herself in O'Daniel's lousy company—not to much of an extent, anyway."

"But you knew who she was?"

"You trying to say I hit on her because I thought she could influence her old man? Well, you're wrong. In the first place, I *didn't* know who she was, not until she told me later, out here; we weren't into last names in Red Bluff. And in the second place, O'Daniel never paid any attention to what she said or did. Hell, she hung that painting of mine right there in their living room, didn't she?"

"Why did she do that?"

"A joke. I thought it was a stupid idea, but she said he'd never notice. And he never did."

"I noticed."

"Yeah. A stupid idea."

I said, "So she and O'Daniel had a lousy marriage."

"The pits. They barely spoke to each other and they hadn't slept together in close to a year. That's why she was so willing the day she met me."

"You were her first extramarital affair, is that it?"

"No. She's not a nun; she'd made it with a couple of other guys since her husband turned off on her."

"What other guys?"

"How do I know? I didn't ask and she didn't tell me."

"But she wasn't seeing anybody when she met you?"

"No."

"You're sure about that?"

"Sure I'm sure. She wouldn't lie to me."

The hell she wouldn't, I thought. Little Miss Roundheels. She'd started up with Munroe Randall, it seemed, while she was already playing around with Robideaux—juggling two separate affairs. And I'd have bet a hundred bucks that she'd been at Randall's house the night he died, plus another hundred that it hadn't been for tea and cakes and a social chat.

But I didn't say any of that to Robideaux. He wouldn't like hearing it, and it might close him off. I said, "What put the damper on her marriage? Originally, I mean."

"He did. Maybe he had something going on the side himself. Or maybe he got wrapped up in being a big shot; he was never home, always running off to meetings, always working late at the office. Or, hell, maybe he just got bored and lost interest."

Or maybe it was the other way around. Maybe *she* was the one who got bored and lost interest, with or without provocation.

I asked, "If things were that bad, how come she stayed married to him?"

"Why do you think? He was making money. Everybody likes money."

"He wasn't making money recently. Northern Development is overextended; that's why they've been fighting so hard on the Musket Creek project."

"I know that," Robideaux said.

"Then how come the sudden decision on divorce?"

"It wasn't Helen's idea."

"No? You mean it was O'Daniel's?"

"He was going to file any day. He told her that."

"When did he tell her?"

"A week ago."

"What made *him* decide he wanted out?"

"He said he was fed up with her sleeping around on him."

"That's all?"

"That's all he told her."

"He didn't try to get her to waive her community property rights, did he? Or to take some kind of smaller settlement?"

"Christ, no. She'd have laughed in his face."

"I'll bet she would."

"Like I said before, she had no reason to kill him. Nobody did. It must've been an accident—"

"Nobody did?" I said. "How about you and just about everybody who lives out here? With Randall and O'Daniel both dead, Northern Development will probably go belly up. That's damned good news for Musket Creek."

"Sure. But I didn't kill anybody to make it happen, and neither did any of my neighbors. I've been here six years. I know these people. None of them is capable of cold-blooded murder."

"How about Helen O'Daniel? Is *she* capable of it?"

"No, and the hell with you."

"You love her, huh?"

"Close enough," he said.

"And she loves you."

"So?"

"I'm just wondering why she didn't call to tell you about her husband's death. You've got a telephone sitting right over there, and she's known about it ever since early this morning."

He came out of the chair, narrow-eyed and tense. "Get out of here," he said.

"It's nothing you haven't been wondering yourself, Robideaux," I said. "Why didn't she call?"

"She's got a reason, all right? Now get the hell out of my house. Otherwise, you and I are going to have trouble, cops or no cops."

He meant it; I could see it in his eyes. I'd got what I'd come for—some of it, anyhow—and I didn't mind leaving, but I didn't want to do it too quickly, didn't want to give him the idea he could push me around.

I said, "Okay. A little warning first, though: If you're holding anything back, protecting Helen O'Daniel or anybody else, you'd better think it over twice. Accessory to murder puts you behind bars a long time in California."

I went out and shut the door softly on its latch behind me. The rain had stopped and there were more blue jigsaw pieces overhead; you could hear the water dripping in the surrounding woods like a chorus of leaky faucets. The heat was rebuilding, so that the air had a wet, steamy feel that was almost tropical.

In the car I sat for a time and thought over what I'd found out. Not much, really. Maybe Robideaux and Helen O'Daniel were in love, but it was more likely he'd been using her—starving artist latching onto a meal ticket—and she'd been using him, too, for stud service. From what I'd seen, both of them deserved each other. Robideaux had plenty of motive for killing both Randall and O'Daniel, but none of it seemed particularly strong. I couldn't see him doing it for community reasons; he was too self-centered for that. His home meant something to him, but it wasn't special enough to warrant homicide in order to maintain it. Ditto his affair with Mrs. O'Daniel. Even if he'd found out she was seeing Randall behind his back, he just wasn't the type to knock off a rival. If he was going to kill anybody in that kind of situation, it would probably be Helen herself.

Mrs. O'Daniel also had plenty of motive for disposing of both her husband and her lover: O'Daniel to get her hands on what was left of his assets; Randall for any one of half a dozen good reasons, including the possibility that he'd been playing around on her too. She *was* the type to fly off into a jealous and violent rage, given enough impetus. But was she really dumb enough to believe she could murder both of them, no matter how clever her methods, and get away with it? All murderers are stupid, Jim Telford had said. Well, maybe. Maybe.

The one puzzling thing I'd learned was Frank O'Daniel's apparently sudden decision to file for divorce—assuming Mrs. O'Daniel hadn't been lying to Robideaux about that, for reasons of her own. O'Daniel had told Treacle he couldn't afford to divorce his wife. What had changed his mind? It was something I would have to check on.

The air was stuffy inside the car; I rolled down the window to let in some of the dying wind. Then I started the engine, backed out onto the road, and headed back the way I'd come.

But I didn't get far, not much more than a few hundred yards. I came around a sharp turn, going fairly slow, twenty-five or so, and on the other side of it was an old black car pulled slantwise across the road, completely blocking it. And somebody, for Christ's sake, was sitting on the hood, somebody wearing a yellow rain slicker and a yellow floppy hat.

There was no room to get around on either side; I hit the brakes, hard. The car slewed sideways on the muddy road surface and the wheel tried to come out of my hands. I held it, managed to get the machine stopped at an angle to the other one, not twenty feet from its right front fender.

Sweat stung my eyes; I sleeved it off and jammed the door handle down and got out yelling. "What the hell's the goddamn idea? I almost plowed into you!"

The guy on the hood stepped down, slowly, and I saw who he was: Jack Coleclaw's son, Gary. The car was the old Chrysler he'd been working on inside the garage yesterday. He covered about half the distance between us and then stopped. Both of his hands were thrust inside the slicker's slash pockets.

He said, "I been waiting for you. I seen you drive by our place and come up here. So I followed you."

"Why? What do you want?"

"To tell you something," he said, and he took his hand out of his pocket. "You better go away and don't ever come back here again. That's what I got to say."

What he was holding was a gun, a rusty-looking old revolver with a long barrel.

I went tight all over; I could feel more sweat come oozing out of me. But he wasn't pointing the thing in my direction—he was just moving it up and down, hefting it. The whole scene was bizarre, a little unreal. For some crazy reason I found myself thinking of Wyatt Earp, Bat Masterson, tough guys with sneering faces saying, "Get out of town, stranger, or I'll fill you full of lead."

"Listen, Gary," I said, quietly, "put that thing away. You don't need to—"

"*You* listen," he said. "I mean it. Go away and don't come back to Musket Creek. If you do . . ." and he moved the revolver again. He knew how to use it, too; the way he was handling it told me that.

He backed up to the Chrysler, opened the driver's door with his left hand, and slid inside. The starter ground, the engine chattered. He put the car in reverse and backed down the road, not too fast, not too slow, until he reached a wide place where he could turn around. Then he and the Chrysler were gone and I was standing there alone in the heat, listening to the rainwater drip in the trees and waiting for my pulse rate to slow to normal.

Get out of town, stranger, or I'll fill you full of lead . . .

When I got back to the Sportsman's Rest there was a dark blue Datsun parked in front of Kerry's and my room, and when I went inside she said, "I rented a car while you were off in Ragged-Ass Gulch. I'm tired of being stuck here all by myself. At least now I can go someplace if I feel like it."

Her tone dared me to argue with her; I didn't argue with her. I went to the telephone instead and tried to call Helen O'Daniel. No answer. I called the sheriff's department and asked for Jim Telford. He was gone for the day, and no, they weren't allowed or even inclined to give out his home number. I looked up his name in the telephone directory. He wasn't listed.

Kerry said, "Martin Treacle called. He wants you to call him back right away."

"Did he sound calmer than he was this morning?"

"No. I think he wants his hand held."

"Let's go have dinner," I said.

So we went and had dinner—a companionable one, for a change. And we came back and I tried the O'Daniel number again and still nobody answered. I read a 1936 issue of *Detective Fiction Weekly*; Kerry read her mystery novel. I wanted to make love in spite of my sore face; she didn't. She went to sleep and I lay there, wide awake, thinking about the investigation and contemplating my lot in life.

At the moment, neither one seemed very promising.

SIXTEEN

The way Monday started off, I knew it was going to be a humdinger.

I didn't sleep very well that night—bad dreams, some involving explosions and fire and hands with guns in them shooting me, then dragging my body down into dark water; others crazily erotic and involving not Kerry but Jeanne Emerson. When I woke up in the morning I felt groggy and my face hurt and the sheets were damply bunched under me. I also happened to be alone in bed: a little fumbling around told me that.

I managed to get my eyes open, to sit up. Kerry was hunched at the dining table across the room, wearing nothing but her bra and panties, playing solitaire. Uh-oh, I thought with a fuzzy sort of bewilderment. Now what did I do? The only times I had seen her play solitaire was when she was angry and upset, and as far as I knew she hadn't gone out anywhere. Which left me—something to do with me.

"Morning," I said, more or less cheerfully. And waited.

Silence. She didn't even look my way, much less quit slapping cards down on the table.

"Hey. Remember me?"

Silence.

"Kerry? What's the matter?"

She paused with part of the deck in one hand and a red queen in the other. Her head came around, slowly, and the look she gave me would have wilted a rose at twenty paces. "What's the matter?" she said. "I'll tell you what's the matter. You talk in your goddamn sleep."

"What?"

"In your sleep. Talk. You."

"What?"

"'Oh, Jeanne,' you said. 'Oh, baby.' And the whole time you were pawing *me* and snuggling up. 'Oh, Jeanne baby.' You son of a bitch."

I was awake now, good and awake. I swung out of bed and got up too fast and almost tripped over a chair that was on that side. As it was, I reeled a little and banged into the wall and cracked my elbow. I wheeled around to face her—the Naked Ape, standing there with his tail and his secret hanging out.

"Listen," I said, "listen, I had some kind of crazy dream, that's all. You can't hold somebody responsible for what he dreams. The subconscious—"

"Don't give me that crap," she said. "I don't give a damn about your subconscious. It's your conscious I'm interested in. Not to mention your conscience. How many times did you sleep with her?"

"What?"

"Jeanne Emerson, the Chinese fireball. How many times?"

"I never slept with her, not once—"

"Hah."

"Kerry—"

"Sure. 'Oh, Jeanne baby.' Sure."

"I'm telling you, I did not go to bed with her."

She slapped the red queen down hard enough to make the other cards jump. Otherwise, silence.

"Come on, now," I said, "this is silly. You can't be this upset over some stupid dream I had—"

"It wasn't your dream, it was what you said. And what you did."

"What did I do?"

"Something you never did before."

"*What*, for God's sake?"

She told me what. I gawped at her a little.

"I don't believe it," I said. "I wouldn't do that to you."

"Not to *me*, no. That's the point. You sure as hell must have done it to *her*."

"Look, how many times do I have to say it, I never did anything with or to Jeanne Emerson!"

"You're lying. You've got guilt written all over your face."

"Goddamn it, I'm not lying!"

"Quit yelling."

"I'm not yelling either!" I was good and mad now, partly because I *was* feeling guilty—and that was stupid because I really didn't have anything to feel guilty about. "I'm tired of all this, the way you've been acting lately. Accusations, mood changes, me having to walk on eggshells around you all the time . . . I won't put up with it anymore."

"You're trying to change the subject—"

"The hell I am. You want *me* to start confessing; how about if *you* do some confessing? How about telling me why you've been so bitchy the past couple of weeks."

She looked away from me. Her face was white, her hands were clenched into tight little fists.

"Well?" I said.

She came up out of the chair so fast she whacked into the table and sent the cards flying. The look of strain on her face was a little frightening. "Did—you—sleep—with—Jeanne—Emerson?"

The way she said that was a little frightening, too, and it took the edge off my own anger. I started to reach out to her, but she backed away from me; her hands were still clenched.

"Kerry, calm down—"

"Don't tell me to calm down. Tell me the truth. Did you screw her?"

"No. I swear to you I didn't."

"Liar."

"I said I swear it to you. She wanted me to. She even . . . ah hell, she came on to me one night, the last time I saw her. The night she came to my flat to take her photographs."

"Came on to you? What do you mean by that?"

"Made a pass at me, what do you think I mean?"

"She came right out and asked you to go to bed with her?"

"No. I was showing her something—"

"I'll bet you were."

"—in one of my pulp magazines, and she put her arms around me and kissed me and then . . ."

"And then *what*?"

"All right. She grabbed me."

"Grabbed you? I thought you said she had her arms around you."

"Hell. You know what I'm talking about."

"No, I don't know. You tell me."

"She grabbed my private part, all right?"

"Your private part."

"That's right, my private part."

"And what did you do?"

"I'm not the lustful swine you think I am," I said. "I took it away from her."

She looked at my face. Then she looked at the middle of my anatomy. Then the strain went away, and color came back into her cheeks, and her mouth began to twitch—and suddenly she burst out laughing. She laughed so hard tears squeezed out of her eyes; she staggered past me to the bed and collapsed on it and sat there cackling and hooting like a madwoman.

"What the hell's so funny?"

"You took it away from her!" Kerry said, and let out a whoop that rattled the windows. "Oh my God! You took it *away* from her!"

"Ha, ha. Big joke."

"What did she say when you tore it out of her hand? 'Oh please, give it back to me?'" Another whoop.

"She didn't say anything, she just left, and I haven't seen her since. Okay? You satisfied?"

Kerry giggled and snorted for another ten seconds or so before she got herself under control. "Oh Lord," she said, wiping her eyes, "I wish I'd been there. I wish I'd seen the expression on your face when she grabbed you."

"Yeah," I said. "Well, it wasn't funny at the time. It's still not funny from where I stand."

"Maybe not from where you stand, sweetie," she said, "but from where I'm sitting I've got a different perspective on the thing." And she was off on another fit of cackling.

I glared at her.

Pretty soon she quit laughing altogether, wiped her eyes again, put on a sober expression, and looked back at my face for a change. "You weren't even tempted, huh?" she said.

"Sure I was tempted. Who wouldn't be tempted? My subconscious is probably *still* tempted, which is the reason for that stupid dream last night."

"You sound angry," she said. "Are you angry?"

"Yeah, I'm angry. I didn't want to tell you about that night with Jeanne Emerson; it's embarrassing. And I don't like having to defend myself all the time, either. I'm tired of being sniped at and treated like a villain."

"Don't start yelling again," she said.

"I'm not yelling, damn it. I'm not yelling. I'm just trying to talk to you here, get some things out into the open."

"What things?"

"You know what things. The way you've been acting, all this moody stuff. What's bothering you, anyway?"

Her gaze shifted to her hands. "Nothing's bothering me."

"Bull. Come on, what is it?"

Headshake.

"Kerry, talk to me."

"I don't want to talk. There's nothing you can do."

Wetness glistened in her eyes again, and her face showed more of the strain. She was hurting, that was plain now. And it made me hurt too—chased away my mad and replaced it with tenderness. I moved over to the bed and sat down and put my arm around her.

"Babe, you've got to tell me what this is all about. It's tearing both of us up, you keeping it bottled inside."

Silence.

"Tell me," I said. "Please."

More silence. But then, just as I was about to coax her another time, she sighed and said, "Ray—it's Ray."

"Ray? You mean Ray Dunston?"

"Yes."

Ray Dunston was her ex-husband, a criminal lawyer in Los Angeles. Kerry had divorced him a couple of years ago, because their marriage had gone stale and because she suspected he was seeing other women; that was the catalyst for her move north to San Francisco. She'd referred to him several times as a schmuck, and in my book that was what he was for letting her get away from him.

I said, "What about him?"

"He . . . I think he's mentally ill."

"What?"

"He gave up his law practice three months ago," she said. "And sold his house and gave up liquor and meat and half a dozen other things, including sex. He's become a religious convert."

"What's so bad about that?"

"I don't think it's a healthy thing, not in Ray's case. He said he couldn't bear to deal with drug peddlers and thieves and whores any more, but that's not all of it. Something happened to him; something happened inside him. His new religion . . . it's one of those off-the-wall Southern California cults. He *chants*, for God's sake."

"Chants?"

"Some sort of . . . I don't know, what do you call it, a mantra? They make their people chant it forty or fifty times a day, no matter where they are. Ray . . . you never met him, you don't know what he was like before. Pseudo-sophisticated, success-oriented, a real three-piecer. And now . . . his head is practically shaved, he wears poverty clothes, and he lives in a commune."

"When did you see him?"

"He showed up at my place about a month ago," she said. "Drove up from L.A. with another member of the commune. It was . . . unreal. Scary."

"Why scary? Lots of men in their forties go through some sort of identity crisis."

"No, it's not like that. I told you—he's *changed*. Completely. He's not the same man I was married to."

"That still doesn't tell me why you were scared. He's not part of your life anymore."

"That's just it. He wants to be."

She said that without looking at me. I used two fingers against her chin to lift and turn her head. "What do you mean, he wants to be?"

"He wants me again. As his wife. That's part of this whole . . . this conversion of his. He's decided he loves me and has to have me back." She laughed, but there was no humor in it. "My God, can you see me living in a commune with a man who chants?"

"What did you say to him?"

"I told him the truth—that he *isn't* part of my life any longer, that he never can be again."

"How did he take it?"

"Not very well. He wouldn't accept it."

"He didn't get abusive or anything?"

"No. He was so calm it was . . . well, that's what scares me. How calm he is. The way he looked at me. His eyes . . . that's why I think something must have snapped in his mind."

I said, "You think he's dangerous?"

"No, he'd never hurt me. It's just that . . ."

"Just that what?"

"He's called me seven or eight times since his visit. No matter what I say he won't listen, he won't go away. He's just . . . there in my life again."

"Change your phone number," I said.

"All that'd do is bring him back to San Francisco. I can't *move* on account of him. I won't disrupt my life any more than it already has been."

I was silent.

After a few seconds she said, "What are you thinking?"

I still didn't say anything.

She said sharply, "You're thinking maybe you should go down to L.A. and have a talk with him, tell him to leave me alone. Right?"

"What if I am? That's what you want, isn't it—for him to leave you alone?"

"Yes. But it wouldn't do any good; it would only make things worse if he knew about you."

"So you haven't told him about us."

"No, and I'm not going to. He wouldn't listen to you in any case, you'd get angry and do or say something stupid, there'd be trouble of some kind . . . oh, God, that's why I didn't tell you about this before. I know you. I know how you brood about things, get them all blown out of proportion, and go off huffing and puffing and making blunders."

"Thanks," I said. "Thanks a lot."

"It's the truth and you know it. You're brooding right now. I can see it in your face."

I started to say something angry—and swallowed it. She was right. But why the hell shouldn't I be brooding? Ex-husband gone whacky and involved in some screwball cult—who the hell knew what might happen. It scared *me*, thinking about it. I loved her; if anything happened to her . . .

"You've got to promise me you won't try to see or talk to him," she said. "Will you promise me that?"

"How are you going to get rid of him, then?"

"I'll find a way. It's my problem."

"It's mine too—"

"It's *mine*, dammit, don't start in now, just don't start in. I'll find a solution to this, don't you worry."

"*You're* worried. Look at yourself."

"I'll get over that; talking about it's made me feel better already. Now promise me you won't interfere."

"As long as he stays in L.A.—all right."

"Even if he comes back to San Francisco. Promise me."

"Kerry, don't try to shut me out of this. I'm involved whether you want me to be or not. I—"

"I *knew* it," she said, "I knew it, you big pigheaded Italian *bastard*!" and she began to bawl.

I sat there. Crying women unman me; two seconds after one starts in I feel awkward and helpless and I can't think straight. All I was able to do, after a time, was to say, "Kerry, don't cry, babe, don't cry," and to put my arms around her and pat her like some idiot trying to burp an infant. She kept on crying against my chest. I kept on murmuring and patting.

Then she shifted position and put her arms around me, and the crying became snuffling, and the snuffling slowly subsided. And then, to my amazement and probably to hers, she was kissing me and I was kissing her back, and other things were happening, and pretty soon there we were thrashing and humping and making noise like a couple of kids having their first big fling.

Yeah, I thought a while later, when we were both still and my head was more or less clear again. Today is definitely going to be a humdinger.

SEVENTEEN

While Kerry was showering I called Helen O'Daniel's number again. Still nobody home. Jim Telford wasn't available, either; he'd been in this morning, and now he was out again, and the deputy I spoke to didn't know or wouldn't say when he'd be back. I called the Northern Development offices. Nobody answered.

I looked up Shirley Irwin's name in the local directory, found a listing, and dialed her number. *She* was home, at least, and she gave me the name of the firm's lawyer, a man named Fulbright who had offices not far from the Sportsman's Rest. He was also both O'Daniel's and Munroe Randall's private attorney, she said.

I asked her how Treacle was holding up, and she said she hadn't seen him since yesterday afternoon and he'd still been nervous and worried then. I said, "How did it go with Lieutenant Telford?"

"Not very well. Mr. Treacle kept demanding police protection."

"Did he get it?"

"The lieutenant said he'd see what could be done. But Redding isn't in his jurisdiction; it would have to be arranged with the municipal police."

"Uh-huh."

She said then that she was afraid Treacle was becoming paranoid. "I asked him if he wanted me to open the office today, and he said no. I'm to say he's out of town if anyone contacts me. He doesn't want to see anyone."

Except me, I thought. I thanked her and rang off.

Kerry was out of the shower and half-dressed by this time. I took my own shower, using cool water in deference to my burns. I put on shirt and slacks, and we went out for a quick breakfast at the place next door. It was another hot day, with scattered clouds but no sign of any more thunderstorms. The air had a vaguely dusty smell again, as if the rain had never happened.

When we got back, there was a message that Treacle had called again. I girded myself and returned his call. He was calmer than he had been yesterday, but the paranoia was there in his voice and in what he had to say. I placated him by saying that I was making headway on the investigation, which was neither a lie nor the truth, and that the authorities were making progress too. Then I asked him if he knew about Helen O'Daniel's affair with Paul Robideaux. He said no, sounding astonished. He also seemed surprised when I told him about O'Daniel's apparent decision to file for divorce.

He wanted me to come over to his condo later, fill him in on the details of my investigation; he meant he wanted me to hold his hand. I said I would, lying in my teeth, and put an end to the conversation.

I left Kerry in the room—and in a relatively good mood; she said she was going for a drive to Whiskeytown—and took my car to the low-slung, modern building that housed the offices of Fulbright and Gault, Attorneys at Law. George Fulbright turned out to be a youngish, solemn, saturnine man with a precise mustache and a precise way of speaking. He was willing to talk, the circumstances regarding his two former clients being what they were; I've never met a lawyer who didn't like to talk, once you got him primed.

He told me that the personal assets of Munroe Randall were "substantial," although he wouldn't name a figure, and that the personal assets of Frank O'Daniel had dwindled in recent months and were now "on the smallish side." He said that yes, both men had made out wills. Randall's estate went to his mother and two siblings back in Kansas; no one locally received a bequest. As for the O'Daniel estate, such as it was, Helen O'Daniel was *not* the principal inheritor. In fact, she stood to inherit only the fifty percent the California community property law entitled her to.

"Who gets the other fifty percent?" I asked.

"A brother in Washington state," Fulbright said, "and a sister in Alturas. Evenly divided between the two."

"Why did he disinherit his wife? Was that provision in his will all along?"

"No. Mr. O'Daniel asked me to rewrite the will several months ago, when it became apparent to him that his marriage had failed."

"Then he *was* going to file for divorce?"

"Oh yes. The last time I spoke to him, two days ago, he asked me to prepare the papers."

"Why did he wait until now? Why didn't he ask you to file months ago?"

"I gathered it was a difficult decision for him."

"He didn't say anything about financial reasons?"

"Not to me, no."

"Do you know if he told Mrs. O'Daniel about his intentions?"

"Yes, he said he had."

"Did she know he'd changed his will?"

"I believe she did."

"Then she also had to know that if he died, and she was still married to him, she'd be responsible for his corporate debts if Northern Development went under. That's the law, isn't it?"

"Why yes, it is."

"And the company *is* likely to go under?"

"I'm not at liberty to discuss that," he said. Meaning yes, it was likely. "But I don't see . . ."

I let him not see; I didn't say anything. I was thinking: Well, there goes her motive for killing him. She got her fifty percent whether he was alive or dead—fifty percent of not much—and that was all she got. And if he was alive, she'd be better off: just wait for the divorce to go through and she could go her merry way without worrying about his business debts.

There went any profit motive for killing Randall, too, because he also hadn't left her anything in his will. Helen O'Daniel may have been attractive and desirable and hell on wheels in the sack, but she wasn't fooling any of the men in her life. Not where it counted, anyway.

Still, there was her probable affair with Randall and her probable presence at his house the night he died. And there was Paul Robideaux, too. She may not have murdered her husband or her lover, but it seemed a good bet she knew *something* about all that was going on.

So from Fulbright's office I drove up to Sky Vista Road on the chance she might finally have come home. She had, but she was on her way out again: when I came in sight of the upper reaches of the O'Daniel house she was walking across from the stairs to where her yellow Porsche sat on the covered platform deck.

I veered onto the wrong side of the road and pulled up alongside her and stuck my head out of the window. ''Hello, Mrs. O'Daniel. I'd like to—''

''You!'' she said, and gave me a withering look and kept on going onto the deck.

Well, hell, I thought. I put the transmission in reverse and backed up until I had the car angled across behind the Porsche, blocking it in. When I got out she was standing there with her hands on her hips, glaring.

''What's the big idea?'' she said. ''Get out of my way!''

''Not until we talk.''

''I've got nothing more to say to you.''

''Why not? You finally get in touch with Paul Robideaux?''

She had, because she said immediately, ''So Paul and I have been seeing each other, so what? That's our business, nobody else's.''

''Not unless it has some bearing on your husband's death.''

''Well, it hasn't. Paul didn't have anything to do with it and neither did I. It was an accident.''

''Was it?'' I said.

''Yes, damn you. Why are you trying to make something more out of it?''

''Because I think he was murdered,'' I said flatly. ''Where were you Saturday night, Mrs. O'Daniel?''

''I wasn't at Shasta Lake, if that's what you're thinking.''

''Where, then? With Robideaux?''

''. . . Yes, if you must know.''

''He told me you weren't. He said he was home alone.''

''You're lying,'' she said. ''He never told you that. He was with *me*, you understand?''

''Is that what you told Lieutenant Telford?''

''It's the truth. Of course it's what I told him.''

So she and Robideaux had finally got together and cooked up a story for mutual protection. That was how it figured; if they *had* been together on Saturday night, Robideaux would have been quick to tell me so. But the lie didn't have to mean anything; innocent people do that kind of thing too.

I said, ''How come you didn't call Robideaux as soon as you heard about your husband's death? I took him by surprise when I saw him yesterday, and that was hours after the lieutenant notified you.''

Hesitation. Then she said, "I . . . was upset, I wasn't thinking very clearly. And there were arrangements to make, the funeral . . ."

"Where were you last night? I tried calling you three or four times—"

Her anger flared up again. "That's none of your goddamn business. I've had enough of this. Poor Frank getting killed, prowlers, and now you again; I've had enough!"

"Prowlers?" I said.

"Yes, prowlers. My house was broken into last night while I was out."

"Was anything stolen?"

"I don't know, I couldn't find anything missing. Whoever it was ransacked Frank's den and then he must have got scared off."

"He didn't touch anything else?"

"No."

"How did he get in?"

"Through the back door, he broke the glass, what *difference* does it make? I'm not going to answer any more of your questions. I don't have to talk to you, you're nothing but a damned private snoop. Either you move your car or I'll call the police."

"Look, Mrs. O'Daniel—"

"You're harassing me," she said. "Move your fucking car or I'll not only call the police, I'll tell them you manhandled me. See if I won't."

I was not going to get anything more out of the bereaved widow—except trouble. I got in and moved the car. She revved up the Porsche's engine until the walls of the platform deck seemed to vibrate, backed out off the deck in a controlled skid, and shot past me burning rubber. I thought for a second she was going to miss the first turn down the road, but Porsches are built for cornering as well as speed; she zipped right around it and roared out of sight.

I pulled out in her wake, driving slow, speculating. A prowler—now what did that mean? Maybe it meant nothing; maybe it was totally unrelated to Frank O'Daniel's death or to anything else in my investigation. But then why had only O'Daniel's den been ransacked? I didn't buy the theory that the prowler had been scared off; she hadn't come home and surprised him or she'd have said so, and there wasn't any dog or burglar alarm or neighbor close by.

All right, then: somebody had been after something specific that belonged to O'Daniel. But what? And who? And why?

EIGHTEEN

I drove downtown again and went through the crowded and shady mall to Penny's for Beauty. The only person in the waiting room was the blond receptionist, Miss Adley. La Belson must have told her I wasn't a city cop; she was not intimidated today. She wasn't even polite. "Miss Penny isn't in and I don't know when she'll be back," she said, and her eyes said: Drop dead, asshole.

So I grinned at her and perched on one corner of her desk and said, "How about if I go back through that arch and tell your customers who I am and that Miss Penny is mixed up in a couple of ugly murders? Can you imagine the gossip? Can you imagine what Miss Penny would say?"

We looked at each other for about ten seconds. Then the blonde made an exasperated hissing sound between her teeth and threw words at me like spittle. "She's at a restaurant down the way. Rive Gauche. Having her lunch."

"Maybe I'll have lunch too," I said, and got off her desk. "Have a nice day, now."

Miss Adley didn't have anything more to say. Her eyes repeated their earlier message.

Rive Gauche was a small, chic restaurant, very French, with colored prints of Montmartre and other Parisian scenes on the walls and waitresses who spoke with Gallic accents that may or may not have been genuine. It wasn't very crowded, and I saw Penny Belson as soon as I came in: corner table, alone, a dish of steamed mussels and a small carafe of white wine in front of her.

She was not any happier to see me than the receptionist had been. But she had more self-possession and this was a public place; when I sat down across from her she didn't protest and she didn't tell me to drop dead, either verbally or with her eyes.

"I didn't expect to see you again," she said.

"Meaning you hoped you wouldn't."

The delicate shrug. "More questions?"

"Some. Go ahead and finish your lunch while we talk."

"I had every intention of doing that," she said. She plucked a mussel out of its shell and washed it down with a sip of wine. "Well?"

"Frank O'Daniel," I said. "You heard about what happened to him, of course."

"Of course."

"Well, like you said the other day, a beauty salon is a good place to find out things. There's been gossip about Mrs. O'Daniel; I thought there might have been some about her husband too."

She didn't answer right away. One of the waitresses came over to the table, to find out if I wanted anything, but I gestured her away. At some other time, and with some other companion, I might have ordered a meal just so I could put it on my expense account and see what Barney Rivera would say. Not today. I kept my attention on Penny Belson's face.

"I don't know what you're after," she said at length. "Frank O'Daniel and another woman—that sort of thing? I've heard nothing like that."

"What *have* you heard, then?"

She sighed. "I suppose the only way I'm going to have any peace is to be frank with you. All right. Evidently he was planning to divorce his wife, sell his house and his interest in Northern Development, and move away."

"Who told you this?"

"One of my customers."

"Which one?"

"I won't tell you that. She's no one you know, no one connected with Northern Development. She is a good customer and I don't want to lose her."

"Where was O'Daniel moving to?"

"The Bay Area somewhere."

"Did he have a business opportunity down there?"

"I don't know."

"Why was he selling out and moving, then?"

"Why do you think? His company is in financial trouble and his wife is a bitch. Isn't that enough reason?"

"Is there anything else you can tell me, Miss Belson?"

"Not about Frank O'Daniel."

"About Helen O'Daniel then. About any of her other affairs."

"She's had several. Would you like a list of names?"

"I was thinking about one in particular. An artist named Paul Robideaux."

It surprised her—genuinely so, I thought. She said, "Robideaux. That name is familiar . . ."

I could have told her where Robideaux lived; she'd probably find it out anyway, soon enough. But I didn't want to have to explain things, and I didn't want to witness the catty pleasure it would give her. I said, "Thanks for your help, Miss Belson," and got on my feet.

"Wait," she said. "This artist, this Paul Robideaux—"

"Actually he's a writer and his real name is Hasselblatt. Thanks again."

I left her sitting there sipping wine and looking coldly thoughtful.

The smells in Rive Gauche had made me hungry, so I stopped at a McDonald's and had a Big Mac and some fries and a strawberry milkshake. Then I drove back to George Fulbright's law offices.

But Fulbright hadn't known anything about Frank O'Daniel's intentions to sell out his interest in Northern Development and move to the Bay Area; he seemed amazed at the possibility. "I can't understand how Mr. O'Daniel could have seriously considered such a move without consulting me," he said.

"Can you think of any reason why he wouldn't have consulted you?"

"No, none."

"Did he have any business affiliations in the Bay Area?"

"Not that I'm aware of. He knew people there, of course—business people. I know two or three myself that I could check with. . . ."

"If you'd do that, Mr. Fulbright, I'd appreciate it."

I made the sheriff's department my next stop, to see if Jim Telford was in. He was. He'd just come back from Musket Creek, where he'd been all day and where he hadn't found out much. He had nothing else encouraging to tell me, either. The police lab had been over the remains of the *Kokanee*, and a professional diver had swept the lake bottom, with the same results in both cases: no evidence to support the theory that the explosion and O'Daniel's death had not been an accident.

Telford hadn't talked to Paul Robideaux because Robideaux hadn't been home, and he was interested in what I had to tell him about my own meeting with the artist and Robideaux's affair with Helen O'Daniel. Still, there wasn't anything conclusive in it. The prowler angle stumped him as much as it did me. And so did Frank O'Daniel's somewhat odd behavior of late.

Lots of possibilities—lots of apparent dead ends.

When I left Telford I drove over to the Redding Police Department and had another, brief talk with Hank Betters. The only thing he had to tell me was that Martin Treacle had been bugging him for police protection and the department, reluctantly, had obliged by assigning a "temporary bodyguard." A waste of the taxpayer's money, Betters said, but it was better that than having Treacle go to the newspapers and build a flap about police indifference.

It was four o'clock by the time I got into my car again. I was fresh out of leads, and I was also hot and tired and my face was hurting some; I headed for the Sportsman's Rest. On the way I stopped to buy a couple of ice-cold cans of Lite beer. The stuff tasted like beer-flavored water, but you got used to it. And now that I was watching my weight, it was a hell of a lot better than no beer at all.

Something had begun to rattle around in the trunk, and when I got to the motel I opened the lid to see what it was. The stone cup I'd found at the fire scene in Musket Creek. It had come loose from where I'd wedged it behind the spare tire. I'd forgotten about the thing—I should have given it to Telford long before this. I took it inside the room and put it on the dresser so I would remember to take it to the sheriff's department later on.

Kerry wasn't there; still over at Whiskeytown or wherever in her rented Datsun. I opened a beer, drank some of it to cool off, and then went to the motel office to see if I'd had any messages. Two calls, both from Barney Rivera. Call back as soon as possible. Urgent.

Trouble, I thought wearily.

Back in the room, I sat on the bed with my beer and put in a call to Great Western Insurance in San Francisco. When Barney came on he said, "Anything to report? Christ, I hope so." He sounded harried.

Well, he wasn't the only one. I said, "Nothing yet. I'm working on it, Barney. I told you I'd call when I had something to report."

"Yeah, well, I'm getting flack here. I'm going to have to bring somebody else in to give you a hand. That's the directors' idea, not mine."

"Terrific. Then we can stumble over each other like Abbott and Costello."

"I've got to do it. The directors want results. They don't want to pay double indemnity twice; that's four hundred thousand bucks—big money."

"I know it's big money," I said. "And if they have to pay it I'll get held responsible and you won't throw me any more investigative bones. Right?"

"Did I say that?"

"You didn't have to. Look, Barney, I'm doing the best I can. Give me another day or two."

"I don't know if I can. . . ."

"Come on. I may be getting close to some answers."

"Okay, okay—I guess I can hold off one more day, kid. Call me by close of business tomorrow, either way."

I sighed as I put the handset down. Getting close to some answers, I'd said. Bald-faced lie. Or was it? Maybe I *was* getting close. Christ knew, I had uncovered a mound of information; if I could only shift it around and make it mean something. . . .

So I sat there for a time, shifting it around—but it was like shifting junk into little piles; none of them amounted to anything by itself. I said to hell with it for the time being. What I needed right now was to go soak my head. In the swimming pool, along with the rest of me.

I stripped and put on my Hawaiian trunks with the hibiscus flowers on them. There was a full-length mirror on the wall in the bathroom alcove; I looked at myself in it and decided I cut a pretty dashing figure for a fifty-four-year-old former fat guy. Still part of a spare tire around my middle—love handles, Kerry called it—but not too much anymore. Slimming down made me look younger too. I didn't look a day over fifty-three.

With my second beer in hand, I walked out to the pool. And dunked myself and swam around trying to avoid a couple of small kids who kept yelling and splashing each other. While I was doing that Kerry came back. I climbed up on the ladder and waved to her, and she waved back and made gestures to indicate she was going in to change. She joined me a few minutes later.

After she'd had her swim we sat in a couple of chaise lounges and she asked how my day had gone. I told her in some detail and with the appropriate profanity.

She said, "A prowler at the O'Daniel house? That's interesting."

"Sure. All I need to do now is figure out what he was after and who he is. Any ideas?"

"Me? You're the detective; I'm just along for the ride. Not too bright, but reasonably attractive and a pretty good lay."

"Pretty good," I agreed. "How about me?"

She batted her eyelashes at me. "Oh, baby," she said, "you're incredible. I see skyrockets every time."

Putting me on again. I sat there feeling wounded.

Kerry fell silent too and stayed that way. Brooding about her whacky ex-husband again, I thought. I took another quick swim, and when I came out she was still brooding. I asked her if she wanted to go to the lounge next door for a drink; she said no, she just wanted to sit there for a while, maybe have another swim.

I went to the room alone, and showered, and as I was getting dressed the stone cup caught my eye again. I could see the fossils on it where Treacle had rubbed off the soot the other night. For some reason the thing held my attention. I stopped fumbling with my pants and went over and picked it up.

Those fossils . . . what was it Treacle had called them? Bryophytes, that was it. Bryophyte fossils, common to this area, etched in different kinds of rock . . .

Rock, I thought.

Rocks.

Things began to stir inside my head. Then they began to run around, tumbling together like little rocks in a landslide. Things I should have added up before. Things that got me a little excited because maybe, just maybe, they were some of the answers I had been looking for.

I finished dressing in a hurry and hustled out to where Kerry sat by the pool. "I've got to go to Musket Creek," I said.

She squinted up at me. "Again? What for?"

"There's something I want to check on."

"What?"

"I'll tell you when I get back."

"Great," she said. "Secrets, now. I suppose that means I can't come along?"

"I'd rather you didn't. I'll be back by eight or so."

"So go," she said, and shrugged. "I'll find something to do."

I went.

NINETEEN

It was a quarter to seven when I came down between the cliffs and back into Musket Creek. The sun had dropped behind the wooden slopes to the west; evening shadows lay across the valley, giving it a soft, peaceful look. Even the ghosts along the creek seemed less decayed, less forlorn than they had during yesterday's thunderstorm. Funny how light and weather conditions changed the atmosphere of the place. I wondered if the people who lived here noticed it too, or if they only saw it one way, in one light.

The car rattled along the road toward the Musket Creek Mercantile. When I got close enough I could see two men standing on the apron near the single gas pump; they were looking in my direction. I could also see that half a dozen cars were parked near the frame cottage in back, among them Paul Robideaux's jeep. The way it looked, the residents were having some kind of town meeting.

The two men on the apron were both Coleclaws—Jack and his son. Gary must have recognized my car, and the imparted knowledge seemed to flare up an argument between them: Gary pointed, jumping around a little in an excited way, and his father made an angry shooing gesture toward the store. When I was maybe twenty yards away Coleclaw shoved the kid, hard enough to stagger him, and then wheeled around and waved a beckoning arm to me. For some reason he wanted me to swing in there—he wanted to talk.

I hesitated, touching the brake. Then I thought: All right, see what he wants—and I cut the wheel sharply and brought the car around to a stop near where Coleclaw was standing. Gary had gone inside the mercantile, but as I got out I could see him behind the screen, watching.

Coleclaw said, "What're you doing back here?" But there was no heat in his voice or in his eyes. If anything, he sounded even more worried than he had the last time I'd seen him, outside the sheriff's department.

"I've got business here," I said.

"What kind of business?"

"You know what kind, Mr. Coleclaw. Besides, I don't like to be threatened. Or didn't Gary tell you about the little meeting he arranged yesterday?"

"He told me," Coleclaw said. "Listen, he's slow, he don't know what he's doing sometimes. He didn't mean anything bad. He wouldn't hurt anybody, not on purpose."

"He had a gun," I said.

"That old Colt? It don't shoot; firing pin's rusted and the cylinder won't revolve."

"I didn't know that at the time. And I still don't like to be threatened."

"You want me to, I'll get him out here and have him apologize . . ."

"No, there's no point in that."

"You got to understand," he said, "feelings been running high around here. The fight with those developers, Randall getting killed, now O'Daniel dead too, and county deputies all over the place asking questions . . . we're all stirred up."

"Is that the reason for the summit meeting?"

"The what?"

"It looks like you're entertaining everybody in town tonight," I said. "Or do you all get together regularly for coffee and cake?"

"What we do of an evening is our business," he said. Something had changed in his manner, and not so subtly; he sounded both secretive and defensive now.

"Okay," I said, "feelings are running high and you're all stirred up. Why not cooperate with me and with the authorities? Why not get to the bottom of what's been going on?"

"All we want is to be left alone, mister."

"Sure. That's what I'm saying to you. Cooperate, get to the bottom of things, and you'll be left alone. Northern Development's just about finished, now that Randall and O'Daniel are dead. Unless somebody with the same ideas buys them out, the plan to develop this area is dead too. It's in your own best interests to help put an end to all the trouble."

He shook his head in a stubborn way and didn't say anything.

In the dusk's stillness I heard the sound of an approaching car, and when I glanced out at the road I saw a Land Rover coming toward us from down by the fork. Hugh Penrose's, probably, I thought. And it was: it came rattling in on the other side of the pump, and Penrose hopped out and hurried to where Coleclaw and I stood.

"I'm sorry I'm late," he said to Coleclaw. "I was writing and I lost track of the time." Then he took a good look at me; recognition put a stain of anger on his tragic face. "You!" he said, and the word was a bitter accusation. "You lied to me the other day, you were just trying to get information out of me. You and that woman you were with."

"I'm sorry about that, Mr. Penrose," I said. "I didn't intend—"

"Liar. Liar!"

Coleclaw said, "Hugh, why don't you go on inside. Tell the others I'll be in directly."

"The meeting hasn't started, then?"

"No, not yet. You go on."

"All right," Penrose said. He glared at me again with his mean, unhappy little eyes and then stalked off toward the house.

"Anybody in particular you're here to see tonight?" Coleclaw asked me.

"No. Nobody in particular."

"They're all inside, you were right about that."

"I'm not here to see anybody," I said.

"Why'd you come then?"

"If you don't confide in me, Mr. Coleclaw, why should I confide in you?"

We exchanged silent stares for a time in the fading daylight. Then, abruptly, he turned and went off after Penrose and disappeared around the far corner of the mercantile.

I glanced over at the store entrance. Gary Coleclaw wasn't there anymore behind the screen. Somewhere out back I could hear a dog yapping—the fat brown-and-white one, no doubt. Otherwise I was standing there in silence, in a ruffly little night wind that had sprung up and that raised a few goosebumps on my bare forearms.

Or maybe it wasn't the wind at all that had raised the goosebumps. I did not like the feeling that was rustling around inside me. There was too much hostility here, and it was too intense. I thought I finally had a handle on what lay at the root of it, but I needed proof, and getting proof meant staying on for a while now that I was here. But not too long. Do what I'd come to do and get out quick and let the authorities handle the rest of it.

I got back into the car and swung it in a loop past the mercantile's facade, so I could take another look at Coleclaw's house. Nobody was visible outside. And if any of them were watching me from inside, the curtained front windows hid them.

When I got to the fork I took the branch that led in among the ghosts. I parked in front of the building that carried the UNION DRUG STORE sign, got my flashlight out of its clip under the dash, and locked the doors. For a moment I stood beside the car, listening. The heavy stillness remained unbroken except for small murmurings and whisperings in the high grasses nearby. The buildings themselves loomed up black and grave-silent—and again I fancied them as waiting things, shades embracing the cloak of night. Then I thought: The hell with that, don't make it any worse than it is. And I went down a narrow alley between the drug store and the meat market, along the path at the rear.

The back door of the hotel still stood hanging open on one hinge. I walked inside. The place had a murky, eerie feel to it; hardly any of the twilight penetrated through the chinks in the outer walls. I switched on the flashlight, followed its beam across the rough whipsawn floor.

The light picked up the skeletal remains of the sheet-iron stove, the steel safe door, some of the other detritus, then finally found the collapsed pigeonhole shelf and the door in the wall behind it. I depressed the latch and swung the door open. Mica particles and iron pyrites and flecks of gold gleamed in the flash beam when I played it across the tier of shelves and their collection of arrowheads and random chunks of rock.

I moved over there. Some of the rocks had designs in them, just as I remembered. Bryophyte fossils like the ones in the stone cup I'd found.

With my left hand I picked up one that looked to be the same sort of mineral as the cup—travertine, Treacle had called it—and pocketed it. Then I swept the room with the light, looking for something that might confirm the rest of my suspicions. The Coleman lantern, the stacks of *National Geographic*, the cot with its straw-tick mattress told me nothing. But under the cot I found a small spiral notebook, and when I fished it out I saw that it was all I needed. It had a name in it, and a crudely drawn map, and together they were hard evidence.

Putting the notebook into another pocket, I turned and started out. The light, probing ahead, showed me nothing but the edge of the desk and the pigeonhole shelf and dim shadow-shapes beyond. I took one step through the doorway—

—and something moved to my right, rearing up out of the gloom behind the desk.

That was the only warning I had, and it wasn't enough. He came rushing toward me with something upraised in his hand, something that registered on my mind as a length of board, and he swung it at me in a sweeping horizontal arc like a baseball bat. I dropped the flashlight, threw my arm up too late.

The board whacked across the left side of my head, and there was a flash of bright pain, and I went down and out.

TWENTY

I awoke to pain. And to heat and a rushing, crackling noise that seemed to come from somewhere close by. And to the acrid smell of smoke.

Fire!

The word surged through my mind even before I was fully conscious. It drove me up onto one knee, a movement that sent pain through my head and neck; I was aware of a numbness, a swelling along the left side of my skull. I had my eyes open but I couldn't see anything. It was dark wherever I was—dark and hot and filling up with thickening clouds of smoke.

Panic cut away at me. I fought it instinctively, and some of the grogginess faded out of my mind and let me think and act. I shoved onto my feet, managed to stay upright even though my knees felt as though they had been vulcanized. I still could not see anything except vague outlines in the blackness. But I could hear the thrumming beat of the fire, a frightening sound that seemed to be growing louder, coming closer.

The smoke started me coughing, and that led to several seconds of dry retching before I could get my breathing under control. I took a couple of sliding steps with my hands out in front of me like a blind man; my knee hit something, there was a faint scraping sound as the something yielded and slid away; I almost fell. Bent at the waist, I groped with my hands. The cot, the straw-tick mattress: I was back in the room behind the hotel desk.

Coughing again, fighting the panic, I slid my feet around the cot and kept moving until my fingers brushed against wood, touched rock—the shelving, the collection of junk. I moved crabwise along it to my left, toward where I remembered the door to be. And found it, found the latch—

Locked.

I threw my weight against the door, a little wildly, half out of control. The wood was old and dry; it gave some, groaning in its frame. I got a grip on myself again and lunged at the door a second time, a third. The wood began to splinter in the middle and around the jamb. The fourth time I slammed into it, the latch gave and so did one of the hinges; the door flew outward and I stumbled through, caught myself against the edge of the hotel desk.

The whole rear wall was on fire. So were parts of the side walls and balcony.

The smoke roiled thickly in the enclosure; each breath I took seared my lungs. There was another smell out here, too—the faint sweetish odor of coal oil. He'd doused the walls with it, all of them probably, so the fire would spread fast and hot . . .

Coupled with the fear and the pain and the smoke, the combined smells made me dizzy, nauseous. I pushed away from the desk and staggered toward the front entrance; tripped over something and fell, skidding on hands and knees, scraping skin off my palms. Flames licked along the front wall, raced across the floor. As old and decayed as it was, the place was a tinderbox: the blaze, fueled by the coal oil, was spreading with amazing speed. All I had were minutes before the entire building became an inferno.

In the hellish, pulsing glow I could see the boarded-up door and windows in the front wall. I got my feet under me again and ran to the window on the left, because a gap was visible between two of the boards nailed across it. The heat was savage here; the burns on my face throbbed, gave off waves of pain—as if all my skin were bubbling up into one huge blister.

I wedged the fingers of my right hand into the gap between the boards and wrenched one of the planks loose; flung it down and went after the other one. The flames were close now, so close that I could feel the hair on my head starting to singe. The smoke was dense, swirling, smothering. I couldn't see anything at all now, could barely breathe; most of the oxygen had gone to feed the fire.

Sparks and fiery embers—little pieces of the room—had begun to fall around me, burning on my hands and clothing. A madman's bellow erupted from my throat: Let me out of here! I tore the second board loose, hammered at a third with my fist where it was already splintered in the middle.

When I broke the two pieces outward the opening was almost wide enough for me to get through. But not quite, not quite, and I clawed at another board, at the same time twisting my head and shoulders into the open space, out of the strangling billows of smoke. Pain erupted in my bad left shoulder; the arm cramped up so that I had trouble moving it. More sparks and embers fell on my shirt and pants, stinging, as if someone was jabbing me with needles. I sucked in heaving lungsful of the night air. I could hear myself making noises, now, that were a mixture of gasps and broken little sobs.

The oxygen gave me the strength I needed to yank one end of the board loose. When I wrenched it out of the way I tried to heave my body up onto the sill—

—but that wasn't the way, wiggle and squirm, that was the way, up onto the sill, through the opening—

—and in the next second I was toppling over backwards, then jarring into the hard earth on my stiffened left shoulder and elbow—*out* of there.

I rolled over twice in the grass, away from the burning building. Got up and staggered ten or twelve paces into the middle of the road before I fell down again. I lay on my back, with the night wind fanning across my face, cooling it. But I didn't lie there for long. Now that I was clear of the fire I could smell my singed hair, the smouldering cloth of my pants and shirt. The smells made me gag, and I had just enough time to roll over and pull back onto my knees before I vomited up the beer I'd drunk earlier in Redding.

But I was all right then. My head cleared, the fear and the wildness were gone; in their place was a thin rage, hot and glowing like the fire, fed and kept that way by the pain in my shoulder and in my head where I'd been clubbed. I got to my feet again, shakily, and pawed at my smoke-stung eyes and squinted over at the hotel.

It was coated with flame, and the fire had spread to the adjacent buildings, was beginning to race across their roofs to the ones beyond. Part of the cloudy sky was obscured by dense coagulations of smoke. Within minutes, that whole creekside row would be ablaze.

I swung my head around, to look up along the road to where I had parked my car. It wasn't there any more.

The rage got thinner, hotter. He took it away somewhere, I thought. Took my keys after he slugged me and drove the car somewhere and hid it.

I started to run painfully along the far edge of the road, back toward the fork. I kept glancing back over my shoulder, keeping track of the fire, so I did not see the cluster of people until I was abreast of the last of the south-side buildings, where the road jogged in that direction.

They were standing in the meadow up there—more than a dozen of them, the whole damned town. Just standing there like a bunch of frigging stumps, watching me run toward them, watching the ghosts of Ragged-Ass Gulch burn as though in some final rite of exorcism.

None of them moved, not even when I stopped within a few feet of them and stood swaying a little, panting, rubbing my bad arm. All they did was stare at me. Paul Robideaux, holding a shovel in one hand. Jack Coleclaw, with his arms folded across his fat paunch. Ella Bloom, her mouth twisted into a witch's grimace. Hugh Penrose, shaking his misshapen head and making odd little sounds as though trying to control a spasm of laughter. Their faces, and those of the others, had an unnatural look in the fireglow, like mummer's masks stained red-orange and sooty black.

"What's the matter with you people?" I shouted at them. My voice was hoarse, my throat hot and raw from the smoke. "What're you standing around here for? The whole camp's burning, you can see that!"

Jack Coleclaw was the first of them to speak. "Let it burn," he said.

"Ashes to ashes," Penrose said, "dust to dust."

"For Christ's sake, it's liable to spread to some of your homes—"

"No, that won't happen," Ella Bloom said. "There's hardly any wind tonight."

Somebody else said, "Besides, there're firebreaks."

"There're firebreaks—that's terrific. Goddamn it, look at me! Can't you see I was in one of those burning buildings? Didn't any of you think of that possibility?"

"We didn't see your car anywhere," Robideaux said. "We figured you'd left town."

"Yeah, sure."

"What were you doing in one of the ghosts? You start the fire, maybe?"

"No. But somebody sure as hell did."

''Is that so?''

''He was trying to kill me, the same way he killed Munroe Randall last week. He damned near broke my head with a board and then he locked me in a room in the old hotel and took my car and hid it somewhere. When he came back he sloshed coal oil around the place and set fire to it.''

Coleclaw said in a low, tense voice, ''Who are you talking about, mister?''

''You know who I'm talking about. The only person who isn't here right now—your son Gary.''

The words seemed to have no impact on him. Or on any of the others. They all kept on staring at me through their mummer's masks. None of them made a sound until Coleclaw said, ''Gary didn't do any of them things. You hear? He didn't.''

''He did them, all right.''

''Why would he?''

''You know the answer to that too. You all hate the men who own Northern Development, so he hates them just as hard. Harder. And he decided to do something about it.''

''You can't prove that—''

''I can prove it, Mr. Coleclaw.''

''How? How come you're so sure he set them fires?''

The reasons flickered across my mind. The stone cup with the bryophite fossils and the wax residue inside; the room in the hotel with the same kind of fossilized rocks on its shelves, a room that resembled nothing so much as a private clubhouse, a room where a child—or a child-man—could keep the treasures he'd collected. Penrose's comments to Kerry and me that Gary was a ''poor young fool, poor lost lad'' and that he had ''rocks in his head.'' A pun, Penrose had said after the latter remark, meaning that Gary had rocks in his head not because he was retarded but because he was a collector of unusual stones. The way Coleclaw had been acting when I'd run into him outside the sheriff's department yesterday; he hadn't been worried for himself, he'd been worried that Gary had killed O'Daniel too and that the authorities would find out the truth. That was why he'd made a point of telling me he'd been with his son on the nights both men died: he wasn't trying to alibi himself, he was trying to alibi Gary.

But I did not say any of these things to Coleclaw and the others; it was testimony better left unspoken now. And I didn't want them to know about the notebook in my pocket, the notebook with Gary Coleclaw's name in it and the crudely drawn map of Munroe Randall's street and property in Redding.

I said, "Where's Gary? Why isn't he here with the rest of you?"

No answer.

"All right," I said, "have it your way. But I'm going to the sheriff as soon as I find my car. You'll have to turn Gary over to the law, if not to me."

"No," Coleclaw said.

"You don't have any choice—"

"The law won't take him away from us," a thin, harried-looking woman said shrilly. Coleclaw's wife. "I won't let them. None of us will, you hear?"

I looked at her, at the others—and I understood the rest of it then, the whole truth, the source of all the hostility I'd encountered. It was not any sudden insight, or even what Mrs. Coleclaw had just said; it was something that was there in her face, and in her husband's, and in each of the other faces. Something I'd been too shaken to see until now.

"You knew all along," I said to the pack of them. "*All* of you. You knew Gary set those fires; you knew he killed Randall, you were afraid he'd killed O'Daniel too—"

"No!" Mrs. Coleclaw said. "He never killed O'Daniel, he never did that!"

"A cover-up, a conspiracy of silence. That's why none of you would talk to me."

"It was an accident," Mrs. Coleclaw said. "Gary didn't *mean* to hurt Randall, he didn't know Randall was home—"

"Hush up, Clara," her husband told her sharply.

Robideaux said, "No matter what happened to Randall, he had it coming. That's the way *we* look at it. The bastard had it coming."

He'd known all along, I realized, about Helen O'Daniel's affair with Randall. Sure he was glad Randall had died. Sure he was willing to be a party to the cover-up. Sure.

I said, "So Randall had it coming. But how about me?" The rage was thick in my throat, like a buildup of phlegm; I had to struggle to keep from shouting the words. "Did I have it coming too? You don't know me, you don't know anything about me. But you were going to let Gary kill me the way he killed Randall."

"That's not true," Coleclaw said. "We didn't know you were still here. We thought you'd left the valley."

"Even if you didn't know, you could've guessed. Come looking to make sure."

Silence.

"Why?" I asked them. "I can understand the Coleclaws doing it, and Robideaux, but why the rest of you?"

"Outsiders don't care about us," Ella Bloom said, "but we care about each other. We watch out for our own."

"More than neighbors, more than friends," Penrose agreed. "Family. No one *here* lies to me. No one *here* thinks I'm repulsive."

More silence. And as I studied them now, the skin along my back began to crawl. Robideaux had lifted his shovel, so that he was holding it in both hands across his chest; one of the men I didn't know had done the same thing. Coleclaw's big hands were knotted into fists. All of their faces were different in the firelight, and what I felt coming off them was something primitive and deadly, a vague gathering aura of violence—the kind of aura a lynch mob generates.

Some of the fear I'd felt during the fire came back, diluting my anger. I had a sudden premonition that if I moved, if I tried to pass through them or around them, they would attack me in the same witless, savage fashion a mob attacks its victims. With shovels, with fists—out of control. If that happened I could not fight all of them; and by the time they came to their senses and realized what they'd done, I would be a dead man.

I had never run away from anything or anyone in my life, but I had an impulse now to turn and flee. I controlled it, telling myself to stay calm, use reason. Telling myself I was wrong about them, they were just average citizens, good people with misplaced loyalties caught up in a foolish crusade—not criminals, not a mob. Telling myself they wouldn't do anything to me as long as I did nothing to provoke them.

Time seemed to grind to a halt. Behind me I could hear the heavy crackling rhythm of the fire. There was sweat on my body, cold and clammy. But I kept my expression blank, so they wouldn't see my fear, and I groped for words to say to them that would let me get out of this.

I was still groping when the headlights appeared on the road to the south, coming down out of the pass between the cliffs.

The tension had been like a silent scream; I felt it end, felt it let go of me, and I said, "Somebody's coming!" in a clogged-up voice and threw my right arm out and pointed. Coleclaw and two or three of the others swiveled their heads. And the tension in them seemed to break too; somebody said, "God!" They all began to move at once. Shuffling their feet, turning their bodies—the mob starting to come apart like something fragile and clotted splitting into fragments.

The headlights probed straight down the road at a good clip. When they neared the bunch of us in the meadow Robideaux threw down his shovel and walked away, jerkily, through the grass. The others went after him, in ragged little groups of two and three. I was the only one standing still when the car slid to a stop twenty feet away on the road.

It was Treacle. And a man I didn't know, a big flat-faced man in a business suit. They came hurrying over to me, and Treacle said a little breathlessly, "What happened? What's going on?"

I shook my head at him. I was still having trouble finding words.

"That fire," he said. "You look as though you were in it . . ."

"I was," I said.

"Are you all right?"

"Yeah. It's over now—this part of it."

"What's over? For God's sake, what *happened*?"

I glanced back at the raging fire. Then I looked up at the line of people trudging slowly toward Coleclaw's mercantile, hunched black silhouettes outlined against the firelit sky.

"Musket Creek just died," I said.

TWENTY-ONE

The flat-faced guy with Treacle was a Redding police officer named Ragsdale—the bodyguard Treacle had been demanding for the past two days. I felt better when I found that out. I did not think there was going to be any more trouble here tonight, but with Gary Coleclaw on the loose, and unpredictable, things were still a little dicey. Ragsdale was armed; that meant we didn't have to get out of here immediately, that we could take the time to hunt up my car.

I told them what had gone down. Treacle did some vocal fussing, but Ragsdale was a professional. He wanted to know if I needed to get to a doctor; I said I was okay, even though my face hurt and my shoulder was still stiff and sore, and explained about my car, and he said looking for it was fine by him. He wasn't willing to go looking for Gary Coleclaw, though, because he had no jurisdiction out here. And that was fine by me; I had no desire to join in on that kind of manhunt. Besides, Gary was not going to get away. He simply had no place to go, not now and not ever.

"Did he kill Frank too?" Treacle asked hopefully. "This crazy kid?"

"He's not crazy," I said, "he's retarded. He only did what he thought the other people here wanted."

"But he *did* kill Frank, didn't he?"

"No, I don't think so."

"He must—must've done it!"

"No. Two deaths, two separate murderers."

And that was the key to the whole complicated business. All of us had assumed that if both Randall and O'Daniel had been murdered, the same person must be responsible. It was only when you realized they were separate cases, with what had to be entirely different motives, that you began to see the shape of things emerging.

Treacle said, "Then who—who blew up Frank's boat?"

"I don't know yet."

There was a hollow, thundering crash from behind us; we all swung around to look. The upper story of the hotel had collapsed in a mushrooming shower of sparks and flame and smoke. The other buildings in the creekside row were a single line of fire. It was like watching a piece of the past—years, events, individual lives—being consumed. All those ghosts . . . if you listened closely to the crackle and roar of the blaze, I thought, you could almost hear them screaming.

I turned away first and went to Treacle's Continental; he and Ragsdale followed. Except for lights here and there, the town had a deserted look and feel. The residents had all shut themselves away now, behind locked doors. A long night for each of them coming up—maybe the longest night of their lives.

In the car, with Ragsdale behind the wheel and Treacle between us, I said, "What brought you out here anyway?" I nudged Treacle. "You're the last person I expected to see."

"You can thank Miss Wade," he said nervously. "It was—was her idea."

"Kerry sent you?"

"Asked us to come," Ragsdale said. He backed the Continental around on the road. "Any idea where the Coleclaw kid took your car?"

"No, but it can't be too far away. Up in the woods to the west, maybe." He pointed the car that way, and I asked Treacle, "Why did Kerry ask you to come looking for me?"

"She was worried because you didn't come back when you said you would."

"Did she call you or what?"

"No. Officer Ragsdale and I were at your motel. I wanted to talk to you again so we drove over there."

"Why didn't she come out here with you?"

"She was just leaving when we got to the motel," Ragsdale said. "She told us she'd been about to drive to Musket Creek—her first priority, she said. But if we'd do it for her, she could go do some other important thing. Mr. Treacle said we would."

"What was this other important thing she had to do?"

"She didn't say. She seemed pretty excited about it, though."

Now what the hell did this mean? She'd been worried about me, but instead of joining in the hunt to see if I was still healthy, she'd gone running off on some mysterious errand. That sounded like Kerry—but it still didn't make any sense. What could be so bloody important?

We were in the woods now; the fire was just a stain on the underbelly of the clouds above and behind us. The Continental's headlights picked up nothing but trees and underbrush until we came to the place where Gary Coleclaw had waited for me yesterday with his gun and his warning. A trail cut off into the forest there, and something gleamed faintly back among the redwoods and pines—a reflection of the headlamps off chrome—and when we pulled onto the trail, there was my car.

Ragsdale and I got out, and I went and looked at the car, looked inside. Gary hadn't done anything to it. Except take the keys with him, but that was no problem: I had a spare set in a little magnetized case behind the front bumper. I fetched them, brought them back to where Ragsdale was standing in the Continental's headlight glare.

"Now you've got your car," he said, "my advice is to report to the county authorities as soon as possible."

"I was planning on it," I said. "You and Treacle should probably come along; you're material witnesses to at least part of what happened here."

He nodded. "Weaverville or the Redding office?"

"Better make it Redding. It'll be easier to explain things to Lieutenant Telford."

"Right. We'll follow you in."

He backed the Continental out onto the road, and I did the same with my car, and we made a two-car caravan back through town. Coleclaw's house was dark; the old black Chrysler was nowhere in sight, nor was any other vehicle. The fire had started to die among the creekside row of buildings—they were blackened hulks now, barely recognizable for what they'd once been—but a spark or an ember had blown across the roadway and touched off the ghosts on that side, so that a whole new conflagration had started up. Nobody here cared about that, either. Except me, a little, but I had too many other things on my mind right now.

Kerry. Where had she gone in such a hurry? And why? I couldn't come up with an answer to either question. Except . . .

"I'd make a pretty good detective if I set my mind to it," she'd declared to me yesterday. And this afternoon she'd said, "You're the detective; I'm just along for the ride. Not too bright, but reasonably attractive and a pretty good lay." Full of sarcasm. But with things going on underneath, maybe—wheels turning, threshing out ideas with her own cockeyed brand of logic.

Damn it, *had* she gone off to play detective?

It was the kind of thing she'd do, to relieve her boredom. Show up the smart-guy private eye boyfriend, out-think him, get to the bottom of things before he does and then give him a nice fat raspberry. Yeah, that was just the way her mind worked.

But that still didn't tell me where she'd gone, what sort of theory she'd devised. What if she *had* out-thought me? What if she'd put something together that I'd missed, figured out who was responsible for O'Daniel's death, and gone gallivanting off to try to prove it? Damn her, didn't she realize how dangerous that could be? She was an amateur; she could wind up as dead as O'Daniel . . .

Easy, I thought, take it easy, you don't know it happened that way. Or if it did, that she's in any danger. She's probably back by now, safe and sound, sitting there in the motel room worrying about *you*.

But I felt uneasy, jittery, and the feeling got worse as the car jounced along the unpaved access road toward Highway 299. I kept brooding, imagining all sorts of things, alternately cursing her and fretting about her. By the time we neared Redding I was a bundle of nerves; and when we came into the city itself I was twitching and twanging and ready to jump all over anybody who looked at me cross-eyed.

Without thinking about it, I put my blinker on and pulled over to the curb. I was out and hurrying back to the Continental before it came to a full stop. ''You go on to the sheriff's department,'' I said to Ragsdale. ''I want to swing by the motel first.''

''Why?''

''My face is giving me hell; I've got some burn medicine there. And I want to check on my lady friend.''

''We can tag along . . .''

''Not necessary. It won't take me long.''

He hesitated. ''You're sure you'll show up?''

''I won't be more than ten minutes behind you.''

''All right, then. I guess you know what you're doing.''

I got back into the car and swung out into the street again. It was after eleven; there was no traffic to speak of and most of the stop-lights were on amber. Within five minutes I was turning in under the red neon sign above the entrance to the Sportsman's Rest.

The Datsun wasn't there.

And the room was empty.

I moved around it, half frantic now. Where had she gone, *where*? There wasn't anything in the room to give me the answer . . . or was there? The local telephone directory was lying on the bed, fanned open: she must have been looking up a number or an address. I peered at the pages. *Q*s. Nobody connected with this case whose name began with a *Q*. She'd probably tossed the book aside after she was done with it and it had fallen open again at random.

I picked it up anyway, and when I did I noticed that one of the pages was dog-eared. Kerry did that sometimes with telephone directories; the one in her apartment had a score of dog-eared pages. I flipped to the turned-down page in this book. *D*s, starting with *DA* and extending through *DU*.

Decker? Tom Decker?

He was listed on the page, all right—Tom Decker, Mountain Harbor, County. I hauled up the telephone receiver and dialed the number, and spoke to Decker's wife, and she went and got him for me.

"Sorry to be calling so late," I said, "but it's urgent. Did Kerry Wade call you earlier tonight?"

"Yes, she did," he said. "Around nine o'clock."

"What did she want?"

"To ask me a couple of questions. First thing she wanted to know was whether or not Frank O'Daniel kept flares on board his boat."

"Flares?"

"I told her he did. Then she wanted to know about his wife."

"His wife. What about his wife?"

"Well, she wanted me to describe her."

"What for?"

"She didn't say."

"Wait a minute," I said. "When did you meet Helen O'Daniel? She led me to believe she's never even been to Mountain Harbor."

"Never been here? Hell, she used to come up just about every clear weekend with O'Daniel, until a month or so ago. Marie mentioned that the night of the explosion, remember?"

I got it then—the one solid lead that Kerry must have figured out. I said tensely, "Describe the woman for me, Tom."

He did. And by the time I put the receiver down, the rest of it was coming together—other bits and pieces Kerry must have picked up on and added together. She'd out-thought me, all right. But maybe she'd out-thought herself as well.

The woman Decker had described, the probable murderer of Frank O'Daniel, was the secretary, Shirley Irwin. And it had to be Shirley Irwin that Kerry had gone to see, alone, close to three hours ago.

TWENTY-TWO

Irwin was listed in the telephone directory—1478 Codding Street, Redding. If she hadn't been I don't know what I would have done. I ran across to the motel office and shocked the woman on duty with my appearance and by demanding to know the fastest way to get to Codding Street. She didn't waste any time telling me; for all she knew, I was a demented person with dark and awful deeds on his mind. And maybe, right then, I *was*.

Codding Street was on the west side of town, near Keswick Dam; I remembered seeing a sign for the dam on my way to and from the O'Daniel house. I charged out of the office and got into the car and went screeching away like Mario Andretti coming out of the pits at the Indy 500.

I drove like him too—too damned fast, taking corners in controlled skids, taking risks. There was little traffic at this hour and I didn't run afoul of any cops or any other wild drivers; those were the only reasons I reached Codding Street in one piece and without incident. As it was I got lost once, briefly, and used up most of the cuss words I knew before blundering back onto the right track. By the time the right street sign appeared in my headlights I was wired so tight you could have twanged me like a guitar string.

Typical residential street, quiet at this hour, lights still on in one or two of the houses. The houses themselves were smallish—bungalows, old frame jobs—with small yards separated by fences and shrubbery. I barreled along to the 1400 block; switched my headlights to high beam when I got there so I could check house numbers and the cars parked along the curb.

Kerry's rented Datsun was sitting smack in front of 1478.

I swung over in front of it, trying not to make a lot of noise that would announce my arrival. I shut off the engine and cut the lights and shoved open the door, looking up at the house. Brown-shingled bungalow with an old-fashioned porch across the front; no lights showing along the near side, but a pale yellow glow behind a curtained window to the right of the front door.

Without thinking much I cut across the lawn and went up slow onto the porch, over to the curtained window. But I couldn't see inside: the curtains were of some thick material and drawn tightly together. I tried listening. That also got me nothing; there wasn't a sound in there that I could make out.

A bunch of things ran through my head: see if there's a window open somewhere, maybe the back door, try to pinpoint where they are first. But I didn't do any of them; I went back to the front door instead, and reached out and took hold of the knob. If it had been locked I would probably have busted the damned thing down with my shoulder or foot. But it wasn't. The knob turned and I shoved the door open and bulled my way inside, through a narrow little foyer and into a combination living room and dining alcove.

And then I stopped. And stood there huffing and puffing and gawping. I don't know what I expected to find in here, but what I was looking at wasn't it. It was not even close.

Kerry was present and accounted for, but she wasn't lying on the floor in a pool of blood, or tied and gagged in a chair, or even cowering in a corner. She was on her feet at the moment but she'd been sitting at a formica-topped dinette table, and what she'd been doing there was counting money. A whole lot of money. Most of the table was covered with nice crisp bills—twenties and fifties and hundreds in neat stacks.

Shirley Irwin was there too. But *she* wasn't doing anything except lying sprawled on a wine-colored couch with her skirt up around her thighs and a big bruise over her left eye. She was out cold.

For the second time that night I felt the sudden release of tension; this time it left me relieved and surprised and very tired. I wanted to grab Kerry and hug her and then shake her until her teeth rattled. Instead I kept on gawping at her, and she kept on gawping right back.

Finally she said, "What are you doing here?" but at the same time

I was saying, "What the hell's been going on?" I started to say something else, and so did she, and I said, "Shit," and she said, "Your face, your clothes . . . what *happened* to you?"

"Ragged-Ass Gulch burned up tonight. I almost burned up with it."

"But how. . . ?"

"Gary Coleclaw," I said. "He torched the old hotel with me in it, just like he torched Munroe Randall's house."

"My God! But what're you doing *here*? How did you know where to find me?"

"Finding people is one of the things I get paid for." My voice was starting to rise; I yanked it down again. "What did you do to Irwin?"

"She killed Frank O'Daniel," Kerry said. "And I know how she did it, too."

"You what?"

"Well, I don't *know* exactly, but there's only one reasonable way she could have done it that fits the facts. That ringing you heard must have been an alarm clock going off—one of those old-fashioned portable ones with a wind-up key. And that pop and whoosh just before the explosion . . . it had to have been a flare igniting."

"Flare?"

"A marine flare," she said. "Standard equipment on all boats; Ray and I used to have some on ours, and Tom Decker told me O'Daniel definitely kept some on board his. Pop the cap on one end and when the flare ignites it makes a kind of sizzling whoosh. It also shoots out more than enough sparks and heat to exceed the flash point of gasoline."

Exceed the flash point of gasoline, I thought. I said, "Then the flare had to have been down in the bilges."

"Probably. Anchored down there, with a piece of heavy string—fishing leader, maybe—attached to the cap. The other end of the string would've been attached to the key on the back of the clock, and the clock would've also been anchored down. O'Daniel had to have been nearby too, either knocked out or drugged. Anyhow, after the alarm goes off on those old clocks, the bell keeps ringing until the key winds down; you know that. In this case, the key also wound up the string leading to the flare, pulled it taut, and finally jerked the cap to set the flare off. Then—boom."

"Boom," I said. But it sounded plausible; it even sounded probable. Damn her, it sounded *right*.

"If you hadn't been there at just that time," she said, "no one would've heard the alarm; no one would have had any good reason to suspect it wasn't an accident."

"There's still no way to *prove* it wasn't. All the evidence went up with O'Daniel and the boat."

"Well, there's a lot of other evidence against Miss Irwin. More than enough to convict her, I'll bet."

"Maybe. Now suppose you tell me what you did to her."

"Well, she attacked me and I had to hit her."

"You had to hit her. With what?"

"Fireplace poker. That's what she tried to hit *me* with." Very calm, very matter-of-fact. We might have been talking about a bad little girl that momma had to spank. "It only happened about ten minutes ago," she said. "I've already called the police. I thought that's who you were when I heard you on the porch."

"Why the bloody hell did you come here by yourself? Why didn't you wait for me? Or call the police from the motel?"

"Oh, don't get excited." Then a pause, a worried frown. "Maybe you'd better sit down. You look awful."

"I feel awful," I said, "and part of the reason is you. Answer me—why did you come here?"

"Because I figured out Shirley Irwin had to be O'Daniel's killer, and I thought there might be some evidence here to prove it. Either that, or I could talk to her and maybe get her to admit something incriminating—you know, manipulate the conversation that way."

"Yeah," I said.

"She wasn't home when I got here. I prowled around looking for a way into the house, but all the doors and windows were locked—"

"Christ, you mean you broke in?"

"No, I didn't break in. I didn't want to do anything like that. I waited in the car for her to come home, and it wasn't until eleven that she did. I said there were some things I had to talk over with her about O'Daniel's death, so she invited me in. Well, she *did* make a slip while we were talking, but she realized it right away. Then she realized I knew the truth. That's when she attacked me with the poker."

"She could have killed you," I said between my teeth.

"But she didn't," Kerry said. "Gary Coleclaw could have killed *you* but he didn't. Survival is what counts."

I was silent for about ten seconds; then I said, "Where did you find the money?"

"In her bedroom. It was in a briefcase—that briefcase there on the table—sitting on her bedroom dresser. Just sitting there in plain sight. The briefcase has Frank O'Daniel's name inside it."

I didn't say anything at all this time.

"She was the prowler at the O'Daniel house last night," Kerry said. "She knew O'Daniel had been embezzling money from Northern Development; I think she was supposed to get a share of it, probably an equal share, but he'd been holding out on her. That's one of the reasons she killed him—for the money."

"Oh it is?"

"Sure. You don't seem surprised about the embezzlement," she said, as if she were disappointed.

"I'm not surprised. I figured that out just like you did."

"When?"

"Never mind when," I said. But it had been back in the motel room, after I'd talked to Tom Decker. And on the way over here. Given all the other facts, it was the one clear-cut explanation for O'Daniel's recent behavior—the decisions to divorce his wife, to sell out his interest in Northern Development and move away; the failure to confide in his attorney about the latter plan. He hadn't been worried any more about letting his wife have her half of their community property because he'd accumulated a fat private nest egg. It wouldn't have been hard for him; he was the company accountant, and he had Shirley Irwin to help him juggle invoices and phony up correspondence. He'd probably started tapping the till when the firm's downhill slide began, which had accelerated the skid and put them in their present financial hole.

Kerry said, "Miss Irwin's second reason for killing him has to be an emotional one. They'd been having this affair for months; she used to go up to Mountain Harbor with him, posing as his wife—"

"Yeah, I know. I talked to Decker a while ago myself."

"But things had cooled down between them; we know that because O'Daniel'd been going up to the lake alone the past month or so. The way I see it . . ."

The way she saw it was the way I saw it: The break with Irwin had complicated matters for O'Daniel, but he'd figured a way out—or thought he had. He must have stalled her while he made his plans to take off with the whole boodle. After all, what could she do once he was gone? Going to the police would have meant a jail term for her too.

But he'd underestimated her. She had tumbled to what he was up to, arranged to murder him, and then gone and hunted up the money last night. Maybe he'd intimated that it was in his house; maybe he'd also let slip at some point where he kept his valuables at home. In any case she hadn't had much trouble finding the stash.

Kerry paused for breath. Then she said, "Don't you want to know what made me suspect Irwin in the first place?"

"All right, what?"

"That anonymous note she wrote to O'Daniel, to begin with. That was stupid of her. She had what should've been a perfect plan for murdering him so it looked like an accident; all the note accomplished was to make everybody even more suspicious of foul play. I guess she knew there'd be some suspicion anyway and was trying to divert it to the Musket Creek residents, but it was still a stupid thing to do."

"All murderers are stupid," I said. "How did the note make you suspect Irwin?"

"It doesn't point directly to her, of course. But I knew the minute I saw it that it'd been written by a woman."

"Yeah? How did you know that?"

"The way it was worded. 'If you don't leave Musket Creek alone you'll wish your mother never had you.' A man would never write something like 'wish your mother never had you'; he'd write 'wish you were never born' or something. It just isn't a phrase men use."

That one had escaped me completely. I sighed and said, "Okay, I see your point. What else?"

"Well, whoever murdered O'Daniel had to be pretty knowledgeable about boats, right? Otherwise, the explosion couldn't have been rigged to look like an accident. So who knew about boats besides O'Daniel? Miss Irwin. Remember when we were all standing outside the sheriff's office yesterday? She said the radio told her the explosion was caused by fuel leaking into the bilges and some kind of spark setting it off. But then she said, 'Poor Frank must have forgotten to use the blowers.' The radio wouldn't have said that. And only somebody who knew boats would know about blowers to get rid of gasoline fumes.

"Then I remembered what you'd told me about Mrs. O'Daniel not liking boats or water, intimating she'd never even been to Mountain Harbor. And then I remembered you'd also told me O'Daniel used to bring 'his wife' up there all the time, according to the Deckers. So I called Tom Decker and asked him to describe O'Daniel's 'wife' and he—"

"—described Shirley Irwin," I finished for her. "Yeah. After which you sent Treacle and his bodyguard off to Musket Creek to check on me and came gallivanting over here and almost got yourself knocked off."

"So did you," she said. "Almost get yourself knocked off, I mean."

"That's part of my job. I'm a *detective.*"

"Are you mad because I didn't come out to Musket Creek myself? Well, I would have if Treacle and that policeman hadn't shown up when they did. But I thought if you needed help, they'd be able to provide it better than I could. Did they?"

"Did they what?"

"Help you."

"Yeah, they helped me. Maybe they saved my life. Ah Christ, maybe *you* saved my life by sending them."

She smiled wanly. "You came here to save *my* life, didn't you. You thought I was in danger and you came charging over here like a white knight."

"White knight," I said. "Bah."

Another smile, tender this time. "Why don't you sit down? You look pretty wobbly."

"No," I said.

"All right, be stubborn. Tell me what happened in Musket Creek, then."

"No," I said, and I went over and eased myself onto a chair near the couch. I *was* pretty wobbly, damn it, and I didn't want to fall on my face.

Kerry followed, all solicitous now, and peered at me up close and made clucking noises. "You sit still," she said. "I'll see if there's anything around here for your wounds.'' She hurried out of the room.

I sat there. Irwin was still out cold, showing no signs of reviving. I wished I was out cold too; consciousness was not too pleasant at the moment—my face hurt and so did my head where Gary Coleclaw had whacked me with the board—and she looked kind of peaceful lying there.

Cars began arriving out front. Doors slammed and people clumped up onto the porch. Somebody started banging on the door, and somebody called out, ''This is the police!''

I stayed where I was. On one wall, a clock commenced to make bonging noises to accompany the racket outside. I looked over at it. Midnight.

Yep, I thought as Kerry came hurrying back into the room, I was right this morning. I sure was right.

Today had been a real humdinger.

TWENTY-THREE

Kerry and I spent two more days and nights in Redding before we were allowed to go on our not-so-merry way. And a few more things of minor significance happened while we were there.

Gary Coleclaw hadn't been taken into custody on Monday night—or rather, Tuesday morning—because he'd left Musket Creek by the time Telford and his deputies got out there; his father and mother had left too. But the three of them didn't get far. The Coleclaws were sad people who had never got far their entire lives, and never would. A Highway Patrol officer spotted them in a diner in Lake County late Tuesday afternoon and arrested them without incident.

I felt sorry for Gary. He was also a victim; guilty of homicide, yes, but not much more guilty than his father or any of the others in Musket Creek who had preached sermons of hatred and violence. It wasn't going to go too badly for him, though: a second-degree murder charge and eventual institutionalization in a state hospital.

I felt a little sorry for the rest of Musket Creek, too—people like Penrose and Ella Bloom in particular. Treacle had decided he wanted no more part of a Musket Creek Disneyland, no more part of land development of any kind; he was folding Northern Development, putting the corporation's holdings up for sale, and "getting the hell out of Northern California." So the residents of Musket Creek had won their fight—except that it was a hollow victory, tainted, and for some, like the Coleclaws, it was no victory at all. Musket Creek really had died on Monday night. And its spirit had burned up along with the shades of Ragged-Ass Gulch. Some of the people would move away now; the ones that didn't would isolate themselves even more than they had in the past, live out their unhappy lives in solitude. No, nobody had won the big fight. In one way or another, everyone concerned was a loser.

And because that was the case, I didn't say much to the authorities about my fear of mob violence that night. Even if I was sure my perception of the situation had been right—and I wasn't, not by any means—it was over now, it was something that had happened, something else that might have happened, it just didn't matter any longer. I did not hate any of those people; I only felt sorry for them.

The one person I didn't feel sorry for, aside from Kerry, was Shirley Irwin. She hadn't confessed—she wasn't saying anything on advice of her public defender—but she was guilty, all right. Her murderous attack on Kerry, the money Kerry had found in O'Daniel's briefcase, Tom Decker's sworn statement linking her with O'Daniel and establishing her familiarity with his houseboat—these all proved it, at least to my satisfaction. So did a careful audit of the company books, which revealed her complicity in the embezzlement. So did the anonymous threatening note, because the authorities had matched the paper it was written on to a pad found in Irwin's house. So did the fact that she could not satisfactorily account for her whereabouts for several hours prior to the explosion, even though she'd arranged an alibi for the exact time the boat blew up. And so did a fingerprint of Irwin's that had been lifted off the back door of the O'Daniel house, a fingerprint that had to have been put there, because of its location, by the person who'd broken in on Sunday night.

Once Kerry and I were allowed to leave, we went straight back to San Francisco. No vacation. We'd both had our fill of Trinity County for a while, and I wasn't in any physical shape to lie around in the sun, or sit around in it fishing. Plus I had lost my enthusiasm for boats.

Things were a little strained between us for a few days, on my part anyhow; I nursed my annoyance at her longer than I should have because of my wounded pride. For her part, she was chipper as hell. No more brooding about her whack of an ex-husband—or at least none that got taken out on me. She went around smiling a lot, looking pleased with herself. Very pleased with herself.

"You know," she said to me once, "maybe I'll do some more detective work one of these days. Now that I'm no longer a virgin, so to speak."

"Not much chance of that."

"Why not? You've got to admit I'm not bad at it."

"You got lucky, that's all."

"Hah," she said. "Lucky. Well, maybe I'll get 'lucky' again on another case."

"What other case?"

"One of yours. In the future."

Like hell she will.

So it was over and everything was back to normal, more or less. Kerry was happy. Barney Rivera and his bosses at Great Western Insurance were happy, or happier than they would have been if they'd had to fork over $400,000 instead of $200,000 to Martin Treacle. Eberhardt was happy; he'd found his missing rich-girl up in the Napa Valley and talked her into coming home. I was happy too, I suppose. I had Great Western's check, and Kerry, and most of my hide intact; my wounds were healing and I wouldn't have any scars.

But there was one thing that kept itching at my mind at odd moments, troubling my sleep. *Had* I been right about the aura of mob violence in Musket Creek that night? Or had it been my imagination, a product of the darkness and the fire and the brush I'd had with death? *Would* they have assaulted me, maybe killed me, if Treacle and Ragsdale hadn't shown up when they did?

Those were questions that would trouble my sleep for a long time, because there was no way now I would ever know the answers.